Discarded Dragons
An Adventure Story

Jennifer M Zeiger

Illustrated

by

Esther Rohman

Published by Jennifer M Zeiger of Zeiger Adventure Publishing

Edited by Darren Thornberry

Printed by IngramSpark

First Edition: September 1, 2021

Cover Design by Justin Allen

Illustrated by Esther Rohman

ISBN   978-1-7351226-2-5

jenniferzeiger.com
jennifer.m.zeiger@gmail.com

Cindy

You pursue your passions wholeheartedly and
encourage me to do the same.

Attention

This book is not intended for you to read straight through! Heaven knows, it'll make no sense if you do.

Instead, read until the book gives you a choice on what to do and then follow the directions to see what happens. Some decisions will lead to success and fame, and others, my dear reader, may lead to misfortune or even death.

Choose wisely for there be dragons within these seemingly innocent pages.

Best of luck!

The Maker hums as he finishes his work for the day. He hangs tools up in a row above the large wooden bench that takes up the majority of the back wall. All the while pushing in drawers with his hip and tossing scraps into their respective containers. Metal clinks in the copper bin, bits of jewel flash in the jewel box, and leather gets folded for cutting later. His strong, steady hands set everything in its proper place.

In the center of the bench lies a half-finished dragon. She's going to be slender and majestic with interlinking red scales and leathery wings, which are set aside to be crafted onto her shoulder blades in a day or two. At the moment, you can't see them around the Maker's torso, but his project of the day involved carefully placing glittering ruby eyes into her metal eye sockets.

The shelves around the shop and storefront are filled with other perfectly crafted dragons but, even half-finished, you know she's going to be something special.

Not all dragons are created equal, as you well know. Some have wings intricately designed so their metal plates fold smoothly against their ribs. Others boast jeweled eyes that sparkle as they see in the night. And still others possess needle-sharp claws that help them perch on the edges of shelves like birds of prey. All these dragons are useful, beautiful, and graceful.

You are not one of these, however. You hide amidst the pile of discarded metal parts on the floor that starts at one corner of the bench and creeps toward the sales counter that sits as an island in the center of the shop. From the pile, you watch the others through a single, murky glass eye. The Maker tossed you aside when he found your thin wings were too weak to carry your body. Months have passed since that day and other discarded bits press down upon your frame, sharing their rust with you right along with their weight.

The Maker's current project holds a lot of hope for you, though. She's small, like you, and many of the parts not deemed worthy of her perfect shape might fit you. One in particular caught your eye while the Maker worked today.

You wait as the Maker finishes putting everything away. Done with the bench, he steps between the discard pile and the sales counter, heading for the front door. You hear him turn the lock and a moment later there's the clatter of the wooden window sign being flipped to closed. He comes back around the far side of the sales counter to peek at his glass Curiosity

Box where it sits on its own shelf near the hallway to the back door. Inside the box are oddities he likes to remember—an Eastern style dragon, a melted dragon, a power-gem fused to a wing. He sighs and a satisfied smile pulls at his lips. Everything's in its place.

On the bench, the half-finished dragon's new ruby eyes glow as the Maker turns out the light and leaves through the back door. Although the dragon is not finished, she can now see the world, especially in the dark.

You keep waiting, watching for those ruby eyes to darken again into sleep. Finally, they dim and a soft snore seethes from her snout.

Only when that snore is steady and no other eyes glitter in the dark do you work your way out of the discard pile.

The shop's wooden structure absorbs the grind of the metal pieces like a sponge but many of the sleeping dragons have excellent hearing. You pause once free of the rubble to see if any of the graceful creatures awaken at your noise. None do.

A thrill makes your metal legs wobbly. Early that morning you watched the Maker toss a green jewel because of a flaw, a small crack, deep within its depths. That jewel would work perfectly beside your murky glass eye and you might actually be able to see the whole room for once.

The tiny green piece lays atop the discard box of flawed jewels at the back of the bench. The Maker will return them tomorrow to the vendor and receive perfect pieces in return. It's tonight or never to make your move.

The other pieces in the box vary in size, but the Maker rarely creates a dragon as small as you. It's hard on his large hands. This is the first time you've seen a gem that might fit for a second eye.

You tuck your thin, useless wings against your sides and step lightly to the workbench, looking up at its height. The jewel box sits atop it, tucked against the back wall that's full of tools. If you climb the drawers of the bench, you can access the box.

Your claws grasp the handles easily but you find the next drawer handle too far away.

Thankfully the Maker finished most of your tail before he gave up on your wings. You turn upside down and reach for the next handle with your tail. Its metal coils encircle the knob with a faint clicking and you haul yourself up, pausing at the next drawer to make sure the sound didn't wake anyone.

Assured, you repeat the process until you gain the top of the workbench. It's scarred from daily use and sharp dragon claws. The red dragon lies only a few feet away, still snoring softly with a thin whine.

The green jewel glitters with ambient

moonlight streaming through the overhead skylight. You tiptoe past the half-finished dragon and grasp that wonderful gem in your claws. Even before you test it, you know it's perfectly sized. Shaking slightly, you snap it into place with an audible pop.

The world loses its dark shadows and turns green to your gaze, beautifully layered in shades of emerald, aqua, and jasper. There's a gray quality to it from your glass eye as well, but this is familiar, comfortable even, and a moan of delight escapes you.

"*What are you doing?*" a voice hisses.

In your moment of triumph, you did not see the half-finished female open her eyes but now those ruby gems burn with life. Her lack of wings and a tail make movement awkward, but she's obviously aware and fully capable of waking the others.

Stuttering, you say, "Cl-cleaning up."

"Not likely," she snorts, opening her mouth to give one of those piercing calls only a small female can.

You hold up your paws, trying to come up with something to stall her. Many of the dragons are vain. They'll curl around a dropped coin or use a gem as a pillow. Perhaps offering her one of the sparkling gems from the box beside you will appease her. But, if that doesn't work, you're exposed to all the perfect dragons and it's a tossup whether you're faster than any of them.

The other option you see is to roll off the bench into the discard heap in order to hide. Rarely will the perfect dragons touch the rust in the heap of metal, so if you make it, you might be safe amidst the rubble.

<hr>

If you offer a gem, go to page 15
If you hide, go to page 97

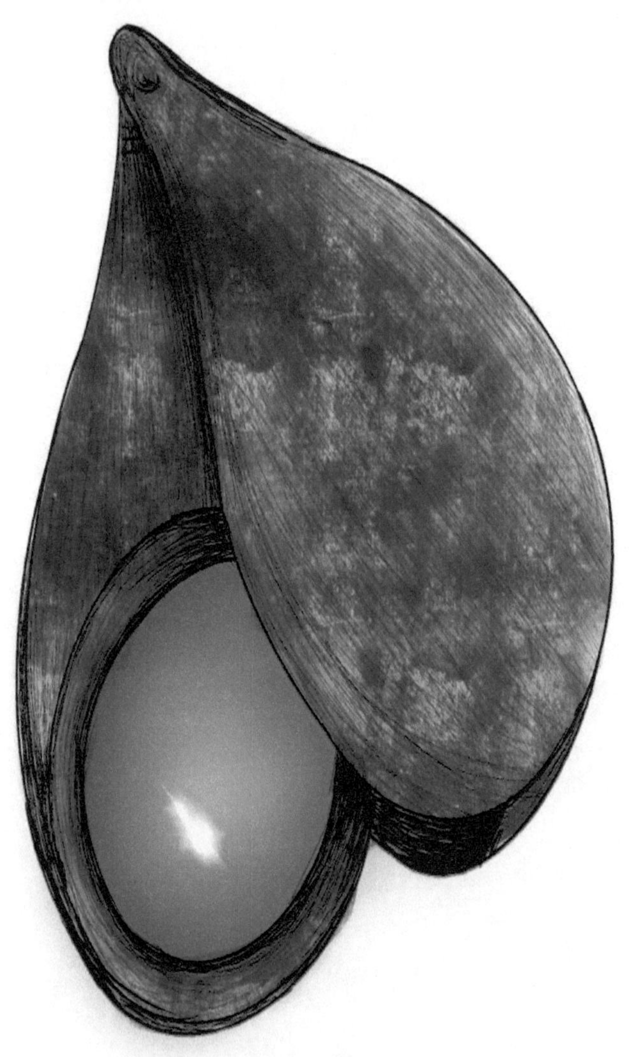

The box of discarded gems glitters in the faint moonlight shining through the skylight, boasting blues and greens and reds of varying shades. You grasp the closest blue, an oval the size of a grape, and hold it out toward the slender, red female.

"This sapphire," you say, "would bring out the fiery shine of your scales."

"That's the box of flaws," she says, eyeing the shimmering oval as you catch it in the moonlight.

"Flaws?" You catch the Maker's loupe, a small round monocle for inspecting jewels, with your tail and draw it over. Inspecting the sapphire, you hum.

The female dragon arches her neck, trying to see.

"There's a swirl," you mutter, "that admittedly would not be great for an eye, but for a necklace, it would be unique. In fact, it would reflect your red in just the right way to make the gem look like it had a red heart."

Your grin is not altogether contrived. The gem does indeed have a faint swirl that, in your eyes, makes it uniquely beautiful.

She doesn't return your smile. "A swirl? If I'm to have a necklace, it should have more than a mere swirl." Her nostrils flare with a huff. "It's ugly flawed, just like you." And she opens her mouth, inhaling and revealing the tiny points of teeth that line her jaws.

Her cry pierces the air and flattens you to the scarred workbench. Your nerves shudder in protest. Not a dragon in the shop could have slept through that siren.

An amber dragon twice your size thuds to the bench behind you, cutting off your escape to the discard pile. With your green eye, he almost looks brown.

Another female with a rounded belly and massive, layered wings coasts down to stand protectively over the half-finished female.

"Thief!" she cries.

You spin on your partial tail and toss the blue gem at the amber dragon's face. Although you're small, your aim proves accurate. The gem smacks solidly against the dragon's forehead just between his eyes.

He rears back with his multi-plated wings extended for balance, all the while blinking furiously to clear his sight. While he's still unfocused, you dart under his wing. You're just about to lunge off the side of the workbench when his tail flashes out, curling around your left wing.

Your momentum is too great and the wing pulls free from your side with a screech of metal and a flash of pain.

With a disgusted "ugh," he tosses the appendage at you as you tumble over the side of the bench in an uncontrolled fall.

You curl into a ball, expecting to hit the discard heap with a shattering thud. Instead, sharp claws bite into the stumpy end of your tail and you're hauled skyward by the amber dragon. His multi-plated wings beat powerful strokes to lift your combined weight.

You scream in anger. The thud into the discard pile would have been better than this. Curling your tail, you sink your own claws into his legs.

He snaps his teeth but can't quite get his head low enough to catch you without unbalancing his flight. Once he reaches the height of the skylight, he drops you.

From this height, you'll shatter when you hit the floor. You grab for a shelf as it spins past but the piece of wood isn't actually attached to the wall. Instead, it's simply set on a few braces. When you grab hold, it flips into the air behind you.

You experience satisfaction when the shelf glances off the amber dragon's side. It dents his otherwise perfect frame.

There's nothing else to stall your headlong fall, though. You cringe, bracing for the impact to crush you.

A heavy whoosh of air gusts past and

you spin in erratic jerks before settling to find you're no longer falling uncontrollably.

You twist upward to see a massive beast slowly lowering you to the discard heap while he cradles your small body in his thick claws.

Once he's set you down, he flies backward awkwardly and lands with a crunch of metal. It's then you see this gray beast is missing several claws, has a heavy dent in his forehead, and can't turn to his left without turning his entire body.

You see this last bit as he moves to stand guard over you.

The amber dragon halts his flight downward and sizes up this new situation.

"Enough, 'Arcus," says the beast that saved you. You can tell he means Marcus but his speech is distorted from the way the dent on his head curves part of his mouth inward. You're surprised that whatever caused the damage didn't finish the dragon completely.

The amber male, Marcus, huffs and tosses one of the discard gems at you.

"Always sticking your dented snout where it doesn't belong," he grumbles toward the beast that saved you before turning away. He settles back onto his shelf, pointedly ignoring the discard heap while he works to remove the dent the shelf left in his side by loosening the screw on one of his metal plates with a claw and pressing the dent from behind.

Slowly, the other dragons settle back in and go to sleep. Even the red gleam of the Siren's eyes finally fades.

When all is quiet again, the iron gray beast picks up the remnants of your left wing and offers it to you with a crooked, almost dopey smile.

"Thank you," you say as you let him fit the wing into place. There's a rightness to having it back that relieves a phantom pain inside of you. The wing's loose now but it helps your balance and makes you feel more complete.

"That was aweso'e!" he exclaims in his distorted speech.

"Shhhh," you caution and you both glance at the shelves full of dragons. Marcus opens one jasper eye. When he sees you're not moving, he huffs again and goes back to his rest.

"Sorry, as 'Arcus recalls, I 'akes 'istakes," says the beast. "I' Blain."

"Blain?" you ask, clarifying as his dent distorts his words.

He nods, setting himself so off balance that he has to step sideways. There's a crunch of metal and a stray bolt skitters down the discard heap.

"What happened with him?" you ask, indicating Marcus with a tilt of your head.

Blain ducks his head. "I hit the shelf

over us with my wings. It squashed us. Took the 'Aker weeks to fix 'Arcus."

You realize what he's not saying. Marcus' brass alloy was worth fixing, Blain's iron was not.

"Least he didn't dismantle you," you say softly.

You both know what you're referencing—the time a dragon knocked into the Maker when he was using his blow torch, thus setting the shop on fire. The Maker dismantled the dragon down to his very claws and no one has dared move in front of him since.

Instead of the reference sobering Blain further, however, he grins. "What are you going to fix next?" he whispers.

You stare at him, seeing the spirit that brightens his golden-yellow eyes.

"Let's rest for now," you say, "while I think on it."

He happily relaxes down into the heap and motions for you to join him. You accept the invitation and take comfort in the solid structure of his wing as it settles over you.

Unlike Marcus's wings, Blain's are solid pieces that don't fold in against his sides. However, what they lack in mobility they make up for in strength. He could easily have carried twice your weight without breaking a sweat.

You think on his question. New wings would be ideal. If you can fly, a world of options opens up for you, including finishing your tail or even leaving the Maker's shop altogether.

Blain starts a slight metallic snore as he falls asleep. He twitches and his claws open and close in reaction to a dream. You stare at the holes where he's missing claws. It doesn't seem like much, but without those claws, his balance is even more precarious than yours.

You sigh. The ruckus you made this night has all the dragons on edge. Going for new claws or wings tomorrow night could be a huge risk with all the Perfects so riled. Perhaps you should simply wait for a few nights.

For new claws for Blain, go to page 23
For new wings for you, go to page 43
If you wait, go to page 139

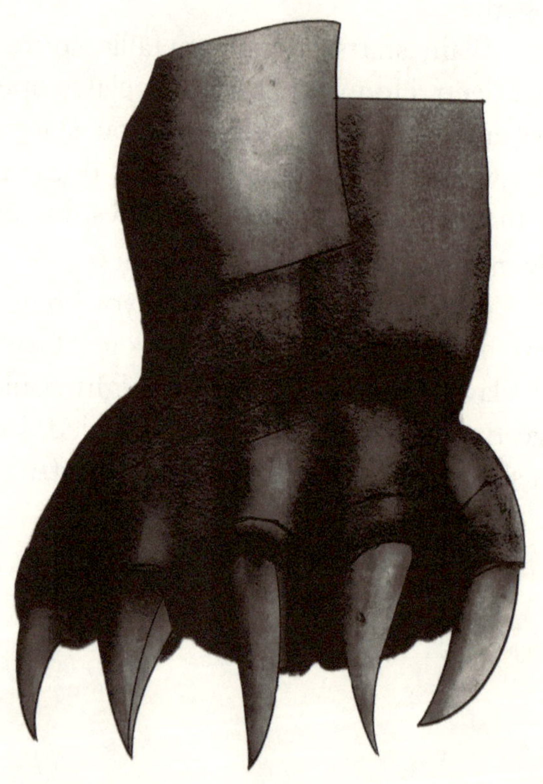

Blain fidgets while he watches the Maker and waits for evening to arrive. His heavy, gray tail shoves a piece of copper down the discard heap, where it thuds against the bent pieces of a folding wing.

He cringes and shoots you an apologetic glance.

You told him your next goal is to find him new claws and, since then, his ability to contain his excitement has been strained to the max. Like a child on his birthday, he'd be jumping up and down if such an action wouldn't draw the attention of the Maker.

As it is, the old man pauses and glances at the pile with a frown. Finally, when nothing seems amiss, he returns his attention to the female's tail, pitching a broken bolt over his shoulder and into the heap as he does.

Although the Maker didn't pinpoint Blain's movement, the female did. After her shriek the night before, you've started thinking of her as the Siren. Her ruby eyes glow, fixated on you and your new friend even as the Maker adds pieces to her design.

Above her, Marcus also watches, curled up on his shelf. There's a faint scratch in his side where the shelf dented him and his claw keeps straying toward the spot like it haunts him. Judging from the narrow gleam in his jasper eyes, he blames you.

The Maker fits the last piece into the female's tail and dabs in a little glue to help hold it in place. Lifting her into the air, he grunts with satisfaction. He lays her back onto the scarred workbench and clamps the appendage in place to dry for the night before he sets about picking up.

He tosses the extra bits of metal into the discard heap and meticulously places his tools in their homes like soldiers in a line. Done with the tools, he pushes in a few drawers and folds his leather scraps into a neat pile before dusting bits of gem into their box. All the while the Maker hums.

The sound of his voice echoes faintly in the room while he finishes his cleanup and locks the door behind him. After the melody of his hum, the shop feels cold, almost hostile, as silence seethes into the wooden walls. The glitter of eyes does not fade along with the hum. With trepidation, you watch shelves upon shelves of perfect dragons.

"Now?" Blain whispers against your ear. You twitch, surprised by his voice vibrating in the metal of your face.

"No," you respond.

He almost whines but then settles back beside you to wait.

The Siren's ruby eyes wink and she huffs in exasperation. Then, slowly, those gems dim until you can hear the soft sigh of her breath in sleep.

Marcus' deep jasper eyes, however, continue to glitter with light from the skylight. He stretches in a feline fashion and yawns but still those glowing orbs remain fixed on you.

Blain trembles with excitement but he continues to wait for your cue.

Usually, lying in the discard heap is easy business but you too tremble with anxiety and anticipation. Your legs begin to ache as hours pass and those jasper eyes never waver.

The giant globe of the moon passes over the skylight and you're just about to give up for the night when Marcus lets out an eye-watering yawn that would have rusted his amber face if he had any tears to shed. He grumbles and slowly his eyes dim to dull, green orbs.

You wait awhile longer but his sides continue to rise and fall in steady rhythm.

"Now," you whisper to Blain.

He sighs and you see the torturous tension that had him fidgeting all day drain out of him as he stands.

The face of the workbench is littered with small drawers holding various hinges, nuts, bolts, molded metal parts, and more. Tonight, you're headed to a drawer directly below the top of the workbench, which holds premade claws. Within its divided interior are claws for every shape and size of dragon.

You follow Blain to the base of the bench and look up toward your target. The discard pile is large enough that you're still standing on the fringes of it as you start your climb.

When you planned together, Blain offered to carry you but after some thought, you asked him to keep watch instead.

So he flies up until he's even with the drawer and waits, all the while watching the curled amber shape of Marcus and the half-finished female while they sleep.

Blain joins you at the bench only when you've reached the drawer and have it open far enough for him to land.

His paws crunch against the metal parts within and he gives a soft crow of delight at the claws displayed before him. His long tail hangs out over the face of the drawer as he starts to test each claw one by one.

You shake your head. "No, Blain. You need bigger claws than those." You push the drawer open farther and select a thicker piece. "Try this one."

He presses it to the hole in his front left paw where his index claw should be. It gives a soft pop as it slides into the socket.

"Ahha!" Blain holds it up, excited.

"Shhh."

He ducks and glances up but Marcus doesn't stir.

Still, you hold your breath for a moment longer just to be sure, but nothing happens.

You select another claw for Blain to try. Again, this one pops into place, a perfect fit even if it is a deep red against his gray.

"One more," you say and delve deeper into the drawer for a thicker claw yet.

You select one and hand it over.

Blain flops onto his haunches and tries to reach for his left foot but whatever injury prevents him from turning to the left also keeps him too stiff to bend forward.

"Here," you say.

He hands over the claw and you test it on his foot. You've got an eye for this sort of thing apparently because it too pops into place. You grin and Blain's golden-yellow eyes glow with joy.

"GAH!" he exclaims as he's hauled backward.

His body is dragged over the face of the drawer and it's then that you see huge amber wings pulling him away. Marcus' claws are sunk deep into Blain's tail.

Before they're too far away, you jump squarely onto Marcus' back. Between your weight and the powerful pull of Blain's wings, Marcus loses altitude and banks left, then right, precariously. He lets go of Blain and rises into the air while Blain flies free.

Marcus' wings gulp air, climbing fast, and you look past his shoulder to see the workbench disappearing below. Cringing, you roll off his back. Air whooshes past and you have just enough time to wonder if you made a mistake before you thud onto the scarred workbench. The slender Siren jerks awake mere inches away.

At the same time, Blain lands beside you and you're both caught in the blast of the Siren's startled cry. It flattens you to the surface of the bench. As she runs out of breath, you realize all sound is gone in your ears.

Marcus lands just to Blain's left and flares his wings in challenge.

Not many sounds would register on your deadened hearing at this point but one clear, single click registers like a bell piercing the silence.

The Maker's arriving for work.

If he catches you all as you are, he's likely to dismantle every single one of you as troublemakers.

Briefly, you think of jumping into the discard heap, but you realize Blain cannot turn fast enough to follow. Either Marcus will catch him or the Maker will see him.

A strong shove might make Blain stumble over the side of the workbench and into the discard heap, but a shove that hard would set you up to take the full brunt of Marcus' attack. It's a sinking feeling when you realize your only other option is to continue fighting and hope for the best with the Maker.

____

If you push Blain, go to page 31
If you keep fighting, go to page 37

Before Blain or Marcus can react to the click of the lock, you dig your claws into the workbench and slam into Blain's good side. You hit him close to his shoulder, which spins him like he's on an axis.

"Hey!" he cries.

There's no time to explain. The doorknob is turning as you back up and slam into Blain again. This time he stumbles. His new claws gouge into the wood of the bench as he sees how close he is to the edge. But you can't let him gain his balance.

You shove him powerfully, one more time. He stumbles and then teeters on the edge, trying to extend his large wings for balance. You keep pressure against his side, keeping his wing down, and he gives a resonating scream as he falls.

There's a crash in the discard heap below just as something tears into your tail. Marcus pulls you close, burning anger in his jasper eyes, picks you up off the bench, and throws you toward the edge.

Your thin wings flare instinctually and for a moment you slow down. Then the loose left wing rips free, throwing you into an uncontrolled spin.

You slam into a pile of small metal bits. Although pain sears through your shoulder blade, you go completely still as the back door opens and the Maker shuffles in.

You realize while the Maker flips on the lights and hangs up his jacket that you landed in the open drawer of claws. High above, Marcus glowers on his shelf. After throwing you, he must have immediately flown to his perch.

Arching your back, you're able to peek out of the drawer toward the discard heap. Blain lays on his left side, his eyes roving over the bench and the drawer of claws. When he sees you looking, he stares. Then, he winks and a grin reveals his teeth. It's inadvisable for him to move so much with the Maker approaching but you can't help but feel a rush of relief.

"Hmm." The Maker's hum wipes away the silence of the shop. "What's this?"

His large, calloused hand wraps around your torso and you're lifted into the air. With careful fingers, he pinches your jaw and turns your head side to side.

"I never would have mismatched your eyes," he mutters. Then, actually looking into your eyes and acknowledging your awareness— something he's never done with a dragon—he asks, "Did you do that?"

Terror seizes you. The unspoken rule about never moving around the Maker has always guided Perfects and Discards alike. The

Maker hums again.

"No matter," he says. "I kind of like the rugged effect." Stooping, he retrieves your left wing from the floor. "But this will never do."

Instead of tossing you back into the discard heap or dismantling you as you feared, he sets you on the bench and gently proceeds to remove your other thin wing.

A few nights later, you peek over the side of the workbench.

"Psst," you call.

Golden-yellow eyes wink open from below. "Did he finish your tail?" Blain asks.

You turn sideways to show him the new steel coils neatly fitted to a point on your tail while you flair your leather wings for balance. He crows with delight.

"You all right?" you ask. This is the first time you've had a chance to talk with him since the testy Siren shared the bench with you. The Maker finished her and now she coils on her own spot in the shop's front window.

"Great!" Blain says, then ducks his head. "Sorry for fighting when you were trying to save 'e."

You scoff. "You had no way of knowing what I was doing. There's nothing to forgive."

"You ingrates!" Marcus growls from above. "Quiet!"

He's still twice your size, but you turn toward him and snap your jaws. He huffs and backs down.

Along with your wings and tail, the Maker added one other thing just that afternoon—a fire throat. He's never added such a defensive mechanism before, but all the dragons know what it's used for. Apparently, Marcus doesn't want to be the first to find out what it feels like to be scorched.

After a moment, when you're sure he won't ambush you from behind, you turn back to Blain.

"Come up," you say. "I think I figured out a way to remove that dent from your side."

The End

Jennifer M Zeiger

All the dragons freeze, uncertain what to do as the brass handle on the shop's door turns.

The frozen moment shatters with the click of the lock disengaging from the door frame. Marcus launches at Blain's left side in a move that looks like he's taking flight.

You toss a small screwdriver at the amber dragon but he dodges away and then banks back.

At the same moment, Blain looks at you, surprised. The move exposes his left side to Marcus' sharp claws. With a flare of his wings, the amber dragon sinks his claws into the gray metal just above one of Blain's massive wings.

Blain howls and his limbs flail in an effort to balance himself.

Using his extended right wing as a ramp, you race up his side and slam into Marcus' chest just as the workshop door swings open.

Always, when the Maker arrives, everyone freezes. The reason for the unspoken rule holds both Perfects and Discards in fear of being dismantled.

But this time, there's too much momentum between you and Marcus to stop as the Maker's leather boots scuff against the rough floor. He flips on the lights just as

Marcus' sharp claws tear free of Blain's back—pulling another howl from Blain—and you tumble with Marcus across the workbench and off the side.

The rule against moving keeps a strong hold on Marcus and you. Even as you fall, you see within his jasper eyes his indecision. The Maker's watching. If he flares his wings to break the fall, the Maker will see, but if he doesn't, he'll take the full impact, including your small weight attached to his chest, on his back. Such an impact is sure to destroy his magnificent wings.

He flares at the last second and your head whips forward and back with the sudden change in speed. There's a crunch as you land against the wooden floor.

Although it's too late, you freeze in the position you fell. Marcus does the same but one of his eyes watches you and there's such a fiery fury in that one jasper orb that you have to restrain a shudder.

Blain's head peeks over the edge of the workbench above.

"*What?*" The Maker's deep voice echoes through the shop.

He lifts Blain from his spot on the bench, muttering to himself as he inspects the claw rents in Blain's back.

"I should know better." The Maker picks up the Siren. "Every time I use that voice box, there's trouble." He holds both Blain and the red female in one of his large, callused hands and bends to retrieve you and Marcus from the floor. Several of your claws are still embedded in his amber chest and so the Maker lifts you both together.

"Such a terrible waste," he grumbles as he disengages your claws. "What a mess."

With all four of you in tow, he heads toward the back of the shop to a small window in the wall beside the door. The hinges for the window are on the top instead of the side. He flips the latch and shoves it open.

"Can't have such troublemakers in my shop," he says and pitches you outside into the trash bin situated directly below the window.

The Siren shrieks as she falls, realizing she's just been thrown away.

"Never going to use that voice box again," the Maker grumbles and the window thuds closed on his words.

She shrieks again.

Blain and Marcus are unfortunate enough to be caught in front of her. They're both flattened to the leather and bits of metal wire in the bottom of the bin. You, on the other hand, landed beside her. You reach out a paw and clamp her jaws closed.

"Enough!" you say.

She whimpers and you let go of her. Thankfully, she doesn't shriek again.

Blain shakes, tests his wings, and then grins. "That was so 'uch fun!"

Marcus scoffs. "*Fun*? That was your idea of *fun*?" He attempts to spread his wings only to find that one of them droops against his side like a metal curtain. Almost directly against the base of the wing, the tendon is cracked from his fall. It sticks up like a broken twig from his back.

He glares at you and takes a threatening step forward. Blain clamps a fully clawed paw down on his tail and actually growls. He's always so happy that the sound shocks you all to silence.

"It's fixable," you say as you shake off your surprise.

"Fixable? You think this is *fixable*?"

You hold up a piece of wire from the trash that happens to be close in color to the cracked tendon. "We might not be the prettiest bunch in the world, but there's plenty of bits and pieces we can find to make ourselves whole again."

Blain nods vigorously. "If the four of us work together, i'agine what we could do! I got claws with only two of us." He holds his claws up as if none of you were around to see how he got them.

The Siren inspects a small chunk of ruby, chipped with a sharp edge along one side, her eyes glimmering. She scrounges a broken sapphire and then an amethyst piece along with a delicate metal cage—bent until one side snapped—meant to hold decorative armor draped down a dragon's forehead. "I could make a one-of-a-kind necklace," she muses.

Marcus stares at her in consternation. You hold out the piece of wire to him, raising your brows in question.

"Fine," he agrees, snatching the wire from you. "But there's no guarantee we'll ever get your tiny wings to work."

You shrug. "We've got a lot of time to try."

As Marcus turns to the Siren for help with his wing, Blain leans over to whisper, "I'll carry you until we find you new wings."

"Let's fix your own wings," you say, reminding him of the rents from Marcus' claws.

He agrees and you set about finding patches for his back. You've no doubt new wings are in your future.

The End

Discarded

Last night, you led Blain into position for tonight's outing. Now you both lay at the farthest edge of the discard heap away from the workbench, almost directly below the first column of hanging wings on the wall. Thus set up, you wait.

Blain's claws open and close, open and close, while you both watch the Maker. His large, gray tail twitches, hitting a solid copper chest piece that's cracked down the middle. It gives an odd twang that sounds inordinately loud.

Blain cringes and shoots you an apologetic glance.

You told him your next goal is to find new wings so you can fly with him. Since then, his ability to keep still has been strained to the max. He's like a child on his birthday, except he's not the one receiving the present. Still, he'd be jumping up and down if such an action wouldn't draw the attention of the Maker.

As it is, the old man pauses, looking at the pile with a frown. Finally, when nothing seems amiss, he returns his attention to the red female's tail, pitching a broken bolt over his shoulder and into the heap as he does.

Although the Maker didn't pinpoint Blain's movement, the female did. After her shriek the night before, you've started thinking of her as the Siren. Her ruby eyes glow, fixated on Blain while the Maker adds pieces to her design.

Above her, Marcus also watches, curled up on his shelf. There's a faint scratch in his amber side where the shelf dented him and his claw keeps straying toward the spot like its existence haunts him. Judging from the narrow gleam in his eyes, he blames you.

The Maker fits the last piece into the Siren's slim tail and dabs in a little glue to help hold it in place. Lifting her into the air, he grunts with satisfaction. He lays her back onto the scarred workbench and clamps the appendage in place to dry for the night before he sets about picking up.

He tosses the extra bits of metal into the discard heap and meticulously places his tools in their homes like soldiers in a line. Done with the tools, he pushes in a few drawers and folds his leather scraps into a neat pile before dusting bits of gem into their box. All the while the Maker hums.

The sound of his voice echoes faintly in the room while he finishes and locks the door behind him.

After the melody of his hum, the shop feels cold, almost hostile, as silence seeps into the wooden walls. The glitter of dragon eyes does not fade along with the hum. With caution, you watch the shelves upon shelves of perfect dragons.

"Now?" Blain whispers against your ear. You twitch, his voice making the metal of your face vibrate.

"No," you respond.

He whines but settles back beside you.

The ruby eyes of the Siren wink and she huffs in exasperation. Then, slowly, those gems dim until you can hear the soft sigh of her breath in sleep.

Marcus' deep jasper eyes, however, continue to glitter with ambient light from the skylight. He stretches in a feline fashion and yawns but still those glowing orbs remain fixed on you.

Blain trembles but, thankfully, he continues to wait for your cue.

Usually, lying in the discard heap is easy business but now you too quiver with anxiety and anticipation. Your legs begin to ache as hours pass and those jasper eyes never waver.

The giant globe of the moon passes over the skylight and you're just about to give up for the night when Marcus lets out an eye-watering yawn that would have rusted the male's face if he had any tears to shed. He grumbles and settles, his eyes finally dimming to dull green orbs.

You wait awhile longer but his amber

sides rise and fall in steady rhythm the entire time.

"Now," you whisper to Blain.

He sighs and you watch the tension drain out of him as he stands.

The wall above the edge of the heap is covered with small hooks holding various dragon parts, wings, chest plates, links for tails, joints for legs, and more. Thankfully, you're headed to that wall instead of the workbench. With how agitated the Siren was the night before, you're glad you don't have to climb up onto the wooden work surface.

You follow Blain to the base of the wall and look upward to your target. Your tail touches the sales counter as you look. Four hooks up, the row of wings starts above three rows of paw pieces and leg joints. Just like with the workbench handles, you find you can grasp the end of the first hook in your paws but the next one is too far to reach without turning upside down and using your tail.

Blain makes sure you can handle the climb before taking flight. When you planned together, he offered to carry you, but after some thought you asked him to keep watch instead.

So he flies up until he's even with the hanging wings and waits, all the while watching Marcus and the half-finished Siren while they sleep.

"All's clear," he whispers when you reach the row of wings.

They hang by small strings the Maker threads between connecting metal tendons. You know immediately just by looking at the first hook that the ones in front of you are too big to attach to your shoulder blades.

You move sideways across the hooks until you see a pair buried two deep that might just fit. An ache settles in your chest at the sight of them. They're interlocking sheets of aluminum beaten to an almost delicate thinness. The gray sheen on them even matches your steel body.

Careful not to clang the wings together, you pull the pair of larger wings from in front of them, gritting your teeth as you hold their weight with your truncated tail, and extract the aluminum set to hand to Blain.

He cradles them in his large paws and flies down to the floor while you replace everything and start your own descent. It's the smoothest night mission you've ever attempted, which makes you a little nervous as you join Blain.

"All's clear," he says again, grinning. You return the grin and turn for him to start working on attaching your new wings. A snort comes from the workbench above and you both freeze, looking up.

The Siren's paw dangles over the edge of the bench, twitching. You and Blain back up to get a better look and realize she shifted in her sleep and is twitching while she dreams.

Blain goes back to attaching your wings. It's a slow process with his large paws and missing claws, but he has them in place just as the lock clicks on the door.

You look at each other with wide eyes. After backing up to see the Siren, you ended up closer to the front of the sales counter than the discard heap. There's not enough time to reach the heap before the Maker walks through the back door. In unspoken agreement, you both go limp on the shop floor. Since you're lying flat against the wood, you feel the vibration of the Maker's steps as he enters, flips on the lights, and hangs up his jacket.

"I've got a wonderful selection," he says as he moves to the bench.

The floor vibrates until a slender, young girl and her father step into your line of sight. As they approach the counter, Blain nudges you.

"Fly," he whispers, staring at the low shelf along the front of the sales counter where the Maker displays his smallest dragons. There's an empty spot there, right at the young girl's eye level.

You check to make sure no one's watching, then push to your feet and with two awkward steps and a strong flap of your new wings, you glide into that empty spot. Elation washes through you at the smooth landing!

The girl turns, her eyes intent as she takes in the shelf of small dragons. Her narrow fingers trace the lines in a blue dragon's snout, then gently follow the arc of a water dragon's flared wing, and continue on to the points of the next dragon's exposed teeth. You smell the faint hint of glue just like the kind the Maker uses, along with the undertones of brass on her fingers, when she curiously touches the end of your stunted tail.

She notices your mismatched glass and jasper eyes, frowning.

In a flash of sudden courage, you wink.

She gasps, but after a moment her expression melts into a grin. "This one, Papa," she points.

Her papa steps over from speaking with the Maker and kneels to look. He's a big man with a red beard that makes it hard to read his expression.

"That dragon's broken, Eira." He shakes his head and stands.

"I'm okay with that, Papa," she says.

He looks back at you and you're tempted to wink again. But even your first small wink had been a huge risk. The Maker tends to dismantle dragons who move in front of customers. He likes his shop orderly and quiet.

But the girl's papa is frowning as he inspects you. If they leave without buying you, the Perfects will make you pay for your daring.

___

If you wink again, go to page 53
If you stay still, go to page 77

Jennifer M Zeiger

From the floor, Blain repeatedly winks one big golden-yellow eye at you. It's now or never.

Just as the girl's papa starts to turn away, you smile a small tentative smile, your internal gears whirring in the quiet, and wink again. Then you freeze, terrified at what you just did and thankful the Maker's behind the counter where he can't see you.

The big man stops and looks more closely.

"All right, Eira," he says, his strong fingers picking you up and setting you onto the counter.

There's a long pause.

"My apologies," the Maker finally says, reaching for you. "This one is not for sale."

"Please, Papa!" the girl says, taking hold of his arm.

Her papa's fingers settle over your spine just before the Maker can pick you up.

"You have a paying customer," her papa says. "How much?"

Again, there's a long pause before the Maker names a price. It's a fraction of what he usually charges for a dragon, but you don't care.

After he pays, the big man hands you to his daughter, who cradles you in her slender hands. As they head out the door, you catch Blain grinning so hard that you wonder how it doesn't hurt him.

The entire way home in the carriage, Eira inspects your tail, then the chinks that make up your ribs, then the connection of your wings. Her inspection remains careful, feather light.

In turn, you stare at the carriage with its thick, purple curtains and cushioned seat. Then you glance at Eira. She has a slender nose just like her slender fingers. Her lips are pursed inward while she concentrates and she keeps pushing back a lock of her chestnut hair that has escaped from her low ponytail.

It's not long before the ride's done and Eira carries you into a brick mansion behind her papa. She heads straight up the stairs and into a room at the end of the hall.

Familiar smells wash over you. Glue, brass, copper, sawdust, iron. Eira sets you on a smaller version of the Maker's bench and leans close.

"So, what shall we fix first?" she asks.

You stare at her. Does she want you to respond? No human's ever tried to speak with the dragons in the shop.

Seeing her expectant look, you say, "My tail?"

The words come out breathy with your unease, but a grin pulls at her lips and she taps the side of her nose as she says, "We'll start there."

Eira delights in creatures like you and her father indulges her interest. After fixing your tail, and then realigning your new wings where Blain attached them too loosely, she starts to make a new set of aluminum claws to match your wings.

While you watch her work, carefully sharpening the edge of a claw, you start to wonder about Blain. You hunker down on your perch above her bench, thoughtful. Eira could do so much to help your friend.

Although you were entranced in your new surroundings when she brought you home, you remember each time the carriage turned. Judging by the way your body swayed and how short the ride was, you can probably find the Maker's shop again. Perhaps you could go back for Blain.

You consider asking Eira to help you, but you hesitate. Her father stated just that morning that he's proud of how she's dug into fixing you and how she's not been greedy and asked for a new dragon already. You suspect trying to buy Blain is out of the question. Which means asking her to help is asking her to steal from the Maker. If she were caught, she'd bear the consequences. It's not like anyone would believe her if she said she was trying to save her automaton dragon's friend.

But you can't leave Blain. Just recently the Maker started muttering about how big the discard heap is and how he needs to clean it up. It won't be long before he throws it all into the trash bin behind the shop.

Eira's not worried about you trying to run away, and there's no reason she should be. So it might be possible to slip out during the night and retrieve Blain without involving her.

You fidget, just like Blain would, wrestling with your options.

If you sneak back alone, go to page 59
If you explain to Eira, go to page 67

You find yourself in a familiar situation, waiting for someone to fall asleep so you can sneak around. Eira's restless tonight with the night's spring heat. Your new claws clutch tight to your shelf above her desk while you watch her toss and rumple her covers.

She's been too kind for you to put her into a compromising situation. Even after the short time you've spent around her, you know she'd help if you asked but you can't bring yourself to do it.

Eira shifts again and buries her head under her pillow. Unlike with the shop's dragons, you can't simply wait for the light in her eyes to dim. It shocked you the first night to realize humans sleep with their eyes closed. So instead, you study her breathing until finally it settles into a deep, steady rhythm. Spreading your wings, you give the girl a last glance before gliding off the shelf and out the bedroom door.

The giant house lies still as you flap your wonderful aluminum wings and coast down the staircase. The front door is closed but the cook leaves the kitchen door open to let the room cool at night. With another flap, you sail over the oven, its yeasty smells and the dozing cat beneath, and then you're out in the yard, heading toward the Maker's shop.

The carriage turned three times, two rights and a left. Reversing the order, you find the humid night air clinging to your metal body. Compared to the dry shop and the cozy house, it makes your joints creak.

It's only after you make all your turns that you realize you never saw the Maker's shop from the front. When Eira carried you out, you were so focused on her face and the carriage that the stone storefronts are a blur in your memory. Although it's dangerous, you swoop down to see into the storefront windows.

There's a dress maker's shop and a cobbler, then a baker, which tells you you're getting close because you remember the bread smell in the Maker's shop any time he opened the door during the day.

A soft clicking sounds on the cobblestones behind you. Although the sound on stone isn't familiar, the sliding of metal against metal is. A glance over your shoulder reveals two glowing orange eyes about two feet off the ground. You're not even sure they're jewels as you've never seen an orange so deep.

The creature stalks you and the glow from one of the street lanterns glints off its black elysium flanks and long, glistening teeth. You've never seen an automaton wolf or elysium before—the black diamond metal is too expensive for the Maker—but you know enough to realize your aluminum claws will do nothing to protect you.

A window ahead glints with watching pinpoints and you recognize the red of the Siren's eyes. The Maker must have finished her and placed her in the front display. You flap hard for the shop but the moment you speed up, you hear the rapid click of the wolf's claws as it gives chase.

You wing higher, toward the rooftops, searching desperately. Behind you, there's a thud and a glance back shows the wolf leapt to the rooftops in a single bound, leaving a dent in the roof he landed on.

"Here, Tasty Morsel," he gloats in a voice so deep you feel the vibration of it in the air. To him, you would only be a bite, maybe two, and then you would be a mangle of crushed metal.

You've heard of automatons like this, who prey on others of their kind, wanting to capture the gem-heart placed within. They collect them like a flesh dragon hoards gold.

The wolf pounces. At the last moment, you bank sideways and his claws only catch a chink in your new tail. The end of your tail rips away but he doesn't gain a solid hold.

"I do like to play," the wolf chuckles and leaps again.

Your eyes snag on what you were hoping to find. The skylight window in the top of the Maker's shop. Sometimes, when the weather starts to warm, he leaves it propped open.

There's a thin sliver of air between the window and its frame. Just enough space, you hope, to glide into the safety of the shop. You flap your wings hard.

The wolf's leap goes long and the canine tumbles over the skylight. The wind of his passing pushes you to the side and you bank hard not to miss the window before hitting the edge of the frame. Clawing it in desperation, you roll through the open gap and into the shop.

A deep voice gives a "woohoo," which is followed by a jarring thud.

You spin to find Blain hovering just below the skylight that he pulled closed and latched behind you. Through the glass, the wolf gnashes his teeth, rending the outside into deep scars.

"Drat," the Siren says from her shelf, "I rather relished the idea of seeing you torn to pieces."

Below, the shop's dragons hover near the windows and you realize your near miss provided more excitement for them than they've probably seen in their entire lives.

"We could still tear them to pieces," says another Perfect. "That one did, after all, steal a home from one of us."

You and Blain share a glance before diving for the discard heap. You hit the pile of metal before any of them can move. Wire and metal and chunks of broken bolts scatter at your impact but the heap is familiar to you and you sink down into the rubble, wriggling until you're lost amidst the rust.

"You really think she'll like 'e?" Blain asks again.

You told him about Eira and since then he can't focus on anything else.

"You're perfect for her," you tell him again. "She'll love getting that dent out of your side."

He chuckles and crunches a piece of brass in his paws to contain his excitement. You cringe. Eira will love him if you can get back to her.

Outside the shop, the wolf still prowls. Every night he checks the windows, his deep orange eyes glowing through the glass, just waiting for an opportunity. Although he can probably break through the glass, he seems hesitant to do so. Perhaps his Maker instilled some self-preservation instincts into him that keep him from harming a human's shop or home. Or perhaps he just views it as part of a game and the waiting excites him. You can't tell but you're glad he doesn't break in.

Within the shop, the Perfects make sure the windows stay closed, and they watch for you and Blain to move. It's been a week and still they keep watch, rotating in two-hour shifts to keep an eye on both the wolf and the discard heap. It's a waiting game.

Eventually, the wolf will find other prey. Eventually, the Perfects will give up watching you. Or, eventually, the Maker will clean up the discard heap and you'll have to make a mad dash to return to Eira. The thought of her makes your chest ache. You never explained to her and now she'll think you ran away.

But you can wait, and Blain, with his bottomless enthusiasm, can wait. It's a game you're sure you can eventually win.

The End

Discarded Dragons

Eira reacts to excitement in the exact opposite way that Blain does. Instead of fidgeting, she plans while she waits for the rest of the house to fall asleep.

You perch on the edge of her workbench as she draws the street surrounding the Maker's shop. You've glimpsed the Maker's dragon sketches but you've never seen anything quite like this. It looks like you're standing at the head of the street, looking past the lanterns and seeing the shop signs sway in the warm evening breeze. Below her current drawing is a layout of the actual shop drawn from your description. Even though the layout is from your memory and you've never actually looked at the shop from the street, it still looks remarkably like you're looking through the front window.

"You're sure the other dragons won't attack?" she asks again.

"No," you admit, "but I've never seen them move when a human's around since the Maker's so against it."

"Good, good." She chews on the end of her pencil. "Then we'll try the skylight you mentioned since it's so warm tonight. I think there's roof access here." She points to an alley beside the bakery a couple doors down from the shop.

With a last nod at her plan, she sets her pencil down and holds out her hand, palm up, toward you. The first time she did this, you stared at her in confusion, but now you step onto her hand without hesitation.

She lifts you up to her shoulder and you step onto the padding sewn into her dress there. Your new talons grip the fabric easily without digging into her skin. By curling your tail around the back of her neck, you settle, well balanced, as she heads down the stairs with a leather bag over her opposite shoulder.

No one moves about the dark house as Eira passes into the kitchen and snags a heel of bread on her way past, but even if someone spotted her, Eira's papa lets her wander the neighborhood for her drawings. She told him at dinner she'd like to go out to draw the moon if the night was clear and he simply told her to be back before midnight.

Still, as you leave the front gate, there's a sense of mischief and Eira grins at you. The night is, in fact, clear and warm and her steps take you quickly down the cobbled streets. You recognize the shop's street from her drawing as she takes the last corner.

"Not far now," Eira says but her voice is soft, perhaps responding to the quiet of the city.

There's a soft clicking on the stones behind you. Although the sharp snick against stone isn't familiar, the scrape of metal against metal is. Eira glances back with you and her hand dips into her bag.

The street sits empty except for its glowing electric lanterns, but your joints tense, knowing there's something that you just aren't seeing.

"Come on," Eira hurries toward the alley with the roof access she spoke of earlier. You keep an eye behind while she grasps the ladder and quickly climbs to the rooftop of the bakery. Just as she's about to mount the roof, you catch two glowing orange eyes in the alley below. You're not even sure they're jewels as you've never seen an orange so deep.

The alley's too dark for you to make out more.

"Something's following us," you tell Eira.

She hums in acknowledgement but keeps going. She's just stepped onto the next rooftop, placing you one away from the Maker's shop, when a figure leaps to the bakery's roof. It thuds onto the wood, denting it, and then straightens.

The creature stalks you and the glow from the moon glints off its black elysium flanks and long, glistening teeth. You've never seen an automaton wolf or elysium before—the black diamond metal is too expensive for the Maker—but you know enough to know your aluminum claws will do nothing to protect you or Eira.

"Wrong. Just wrong," Eira grumbles, seeing it. She sounds more angry than scared although the wolf is almost two feet tall. She turns to face it. "Go see if the shop skylight is open," she instructs. "If it is, call for your friend."

You hesitate, not wanting to leave her to face the wolf alone. You've heard of automatons like this, who prey on others of their kind, wanting to capture the gem-heart placed within. They collect them like a flesh dragon hoards gold, but it never occurred to you such an automaton would approach a human.

"Go!" Eira insists.

You spread your wings and take flight.

Instantly, the wolf pounces but Eira steps in the way, her hand coming out of her bag with a baton that extends with a sharp snap. The baton catches the wolf in the chest, clanging with a deep boom.

You wing hard for the Maker's shop and see, in relief, that he propped the skylight open as he sometimes does to air out the shop on warm nights. As you skip to a stop, flaring your wings to catch the skylight frame in your claws, you see the wolf stand back up from where the baton smashed him to the roof.

There's not a scratch on him and you realize, with his elysium frame, Eira's baton can't hurt him, just throw him around.

Eira seems to comprehend this, too. When the wolf grins at her, she grins right back but there's a tremble to her hand now. Your chest swells with pride although you regret getting her into this mess. You're amazed that her papa's okay with her wandering the city at night with such automatons running loose.

"I'll get two tasty morsels tonight," the wolf gloats.

Eira doesn't respond. Instead, her finger clicks something on the baton and it comes to life, glowing with its own kind of dark fire.

The wolf hesitates.

From below you in the shop, you hear a rustling. It pulls you back to your own part of this mission and you call, "Blain? Blain, fly up to the window."

Two golden-yellow eyes blink open far below and a large dragon shakes himself from the discard heap.

"You're back!" Blain exclaims and takes flight, his powerful wings eating up the distance with ease.

Something darts across the workbench and flies toward him.

"Watch out!" you shout

Blain can't turn fast enough to avoid whoever gave chase. The creature latches onto Blain's tail and when he turns, trying to see his attacker, you catch the tiny blue eyes of a dragon holding on with his metal limbs trembling in strain. It has no wings. The tiny dragon didn't fly at Blain. It jumped.

"Blain, don't fight him," you say. "Just fly."

He gives up trying to see what's hanging onto him and flaps hard toward the skylight. When he gets close enough, you help him slide through the gap, pulling the tiny blue dragon along with him.

"EEEK!" the creature screeches when he sees Eira and the wolf.

The rooftop on which they stand is now littered with chunks of wood torn up by the wolf's claws. The beast swipes at Eira's legs. She skips back and swings, catching the paw. It's not a hard swing, but on contact, the baton zaps and the wolf flinches.

"Its tail!" Eira shouts to you. "Go for its tail."

Your brain doesn't process why she wants you to attack a creature five times your size, but it doesn't matter. You got her into this and you're not leaving her to the wolf. You launch into flight and find Blain beside you. He goes left while you go right to catch the wolf from the sides.

Blain misses catching the long black tail as the wolf spins and snarls at him but you see the bunching of the canine's muscles and anticipate the spin. So as the wolf turns, you sink your claws between the plates of elysium, knowing you can't puncture the metal itself. The plates pull apart, gaping just enough to admit your claws.

"Pull hard!" Eira shouts at the same time as she swings.

You sink your claws in deep and give a single powerful backward flap of your small wings even as the wolf whips you around in the air.

Eira's baton comes down, hitting the gap in the plates.

ZAP!

Your teeth feel like you scraped your claws across a chalkboard. Blinking, you stare up into Blain's golden-yellow eyes. You lost your grip on the wolf's tail somewhere along the line and now, you see, you're lying on the rooftop like a spineless automaton.

"You're awake!" Blain says.

Eira gives a deep sigh. "Good. I hoped most of the jolt hit the wolf, but it was a risk."

"Where's the wolf?" you ask.

"That last zap went into his innards," Eira explains. "It shut him down and he rolled off the roof."

Perhaps Eira's papa isn't crazy after all.

From amidst Eira's loose hair where it drapes her shoulder, you see tiny blue eyes peeking out.

"Well, hello," you say.

The little dragon shrinks back and Eira chuckles.

"Looks like you started something," she says, picking you and then Blain up and depositing you both into her shoulder bag. "You gave this little one the courage to flee the discard heap as well. It'll be a challenge to make him wings. It's a wonder your Maker got him as far along as he did with how tiny his frame is, but maybe with your thin claws, we can manage it."

You and Blain share a grin and, for once, you find yourself just as excited as your friend.

The End

From the floor, Blain repeatedly winks one big golden-yellow eye at you, but you remember the last time the Maker thought a dragon moved in front of a customer. He disassembled the creature down to its gem-heart.

The girl's papa shakes his head and turns away. Your heart sinks as the girl follows him. They peruse the other dragons but eventually leave without buying any.

The Maker huffs, frustrated at the lack of a sale so much that he doesn't round the counter to see which dragon's broken. He goes to work finishing the Siren and eventually his deep hum returns.

It's the only pleasant thing throughout the day because, as time passes from morning to noon and on toward evening, you become more and more aware of the angry glares of the Perfects.

The shelf you now sit on places you in amongst them all. To the right and left are a fat, green male and a long blue female, both small, but terribly close. If you could sweat, it would be running down your face in the heat of the shop.

Blain notices their looks as well and starts to inch closer and closer across the floor like he might protect you. Against one dragon, he'd be fine, but there are so many Perfects now eyeing you that there's no way you'll both survive if they decide to take out their anger.

The light fades with the day and the Maker returns his tools to where they hang above the bench. His motions are so familiar that you imagine him folding pieces of leather and tossing flawed gems into the return box on the bench.

Then he retrieves a stool and a long-handled broom. Standing on the three-legged seat, he nudges the latch on the skylight open with the broom and props the glass open a crack. A warm breeze wafts into the shop, carrying the yeasty flavor of baked bread from a nearby shop.

Apparently, the heat isn't only coming from the Perfects' angry looks. It must be spring, you realize, because the Maker only opens the skylight in warmer weather.

Finishing up, the Maker replaces the broom and stool and heads out.

The shop goes quiet for half a moment before Blain leaps off the floor to block the blue female on your right just as she starts to turn. He swats her from the shelf with a heavy paw.

You spin to catch the green male on the other side, but you only have enough time to brace before he runs into you. He's small but heavy and he bowls you over. Tumbling head over tail, you flip off the shelf and crash against the floor on your spine.

You haven't the instinct yet to flare your new aluminum wings to slow your fall. This saves the connections along your shoulder blades from being crushed when you land.

"Fly," Blain shouts.

Watching the green dragon waddle toward you, you understand Blain's intent. The dragon's so heavy that his wings are useless for anything but short hops.

Flipping onto your feet, you truly take flight for the first time in your life. It's marvelous, and ends as quickly as it starts.

"No, 'Arcus!"

You look back at Blain's distorted shout in time to see a Perfect amber dragon swoop toward you. He snatches you out of the air with his long claws.

Those claws circle around your neck and he roars in triumph. He climbs, each powerful flap of his magnificent amber wings pulling at your neck and carrying you past dozens of airborne dragons.

Below, you hear a ruckus and figure Blain's trying to reach you, but there's no way he'll get through so many.

You're near the ceiling when a different noise, a sharp splintering of wood, makes the amber male, Marcus, pause in flight. You both look up.

The skylight—glass, frame, and hinges—is gone, torn away in a single piece. In its place glow the deep orange eyes of an automaton wolf whose shoulders barely fit through the narrow window frame. Black teeth glisten when the wolf grins down at the dragons in the shop.

"I'll enjoy a feast tonight," he growls and leaps for the closest dragons—Marcus and you.

Marcus drops you, and you fall like a chunk of granite until reason returns and you flare your new wings. They catch air with a whoop just before you hit the top of the workbench. It's enough to keep you from snapping your legs.

Seconds later, the wolf thuds onto the bench with Marcus' amber body in his teeth. Dozens of dragons attack him, their claws screeching against the wolf's sides. He flinches, but when the dragons pull away, there's not a scratch on him.

He's made of elysium, you realize. Not a claw in the shop can puncture his diamond metal. He spits Marcus onto the bench and thumps a paw onto his chest to hold him. Grinning, his index claw scraps against Marcus' metal chest plates, pulling at the edges right over the gem-heart.

You've heard of automatons like this, who prey on others of their kind, wanting to capture the gem-heart placed within. They collect them like a flesh dragon hoards gold. If something's not done, he'll tear through all the dragons in the shop.

At the back of the workbench, the Maker's tools glint in the silvery moonlight coming through the broken skylight.

The wolf's now sitting on his haunches, gloating over his prey even as the other dragons attack his eyes and tail and sides. He's got all the time in the world to enjoy his game.

From your vantage point, you can ·see the tiny screws in his chest plates. You can't get through the elysium, but maybe you can detach it, exposing the wolf's own gem-heart. It'd require you to slide underneath the beast's chest and loosen the screws before the wolf crushes you.

The only other option you see is distracting him. You know where the Maker keeps his gem-hearts for new dragons. If you hold one in your paws, the wolf might think the taking's easy and chase you back out the skylight. You're light and fast, but you have no way of knowing if the wolf is faster.

If you attack, go to page 83
If you entice the wolf to chase you, go to page 89

The Maker's tools are heavier than you anticipated. When you free a screwdriver and chisel from their hooks, they fall out of your paws, thudding to the top of the workbench. In the commotion, no one but Blain notices.

His golden-yellow eyes are nearly popping out of his skull as he lands beside you.

"What's the 'lan?" he asks.

"Gem-heart," is all you can think to say as you lift the tools.

"His?" Blain squeaks.

"Yup," you respond. "Distract him for me." And you scramble across the bench toward where the wolf has Marcus' chest plate peeled back. Inside glints a perfectly round amber gem the size of a grape.

By now the wolf would be salivating if he could. The gleam in his orange eyes makes your own gem-heart squeeze in terror.

There's a scraping of claws behind you and your terror eases a fraction, knowing Blain's helping.

Cringing at what you're about to do, you hold the tools tight to your chest and dive sideways, skidding to a stop below the beast's chest.

The canine arches his neck to look at the small dragon now braced against his chest plates, a sneer pulling up the metal around his teeth. He only gets a moment to look at you, however, before Blain slams into the side of his head.

It doesn't move the wolf's body, but Blain's made of iron and the impact whips the wolf's muzzle sideways.

Marcus jerks suddenly, dislodging the paw holding him to the workbench. You expect him to flee since his gem-heart's exposed. He meets your eyes for a second, taking in the tools you're lifting toward the screws in the wolf's chest.

With a nod and a powerful flap of his wings, he launches off the bench and smashes into the wolf's chin just as the beast is recovering from Blain's attack. There's a crunch of metal—part of Marcus' head and shoulder caving in—and the wolf's head snaps upward.

An aggravated growl rumbles out of the beast. You feel it in the screwdriver as you spin the head of a tiny screw free from the elysium. It clatters against your head as it falls but you move to the next screw without pausing.

Two screws and you can probably pry the plates back enough to slide inside the wolf's chest. The second screw sticks. You groan, clamping both paws around the screwdriver handle. Heaving on it, the screw breaks loose.

Other dragons have caught onto what you're attempting by now. With surprise, you catch sight of the slender Siren. She lands and opens her jaws, exposing her voice box with a deep breath. You have a bare second to grab hold of the loose chest plates before she lets out a scream that pierces the air.

The Siren's wail vibrates through every piece of the wolf in a shudder so violent your weight on the plates pulls them open farther. The wolf's shocked into stillness, which gives you just enough time to wedge yourself headfirst into the gap in his chest, the chisel held tight in your paw.

One shove of your hind legs, claws digging into the wood of the workbench for purchase, and you're inside the wolf's chest cavity. He shudders mightily. Your paws slide around, screeching against the inside of the elysium.

He shudders again and you use the motion to slide toward the glowing, deep orange gem-heart. It's cradled in a delicate metal cage made of wires running top to bottom. When you grab ahold, your claws mar it, scoring the copper by bending it out of its perfectly straight lines. You force the tiny points of your claws between one wire and the glowing gem-heart. It takes only a little effort to shove the chisel into the gap.

The wolf convulses like he feels the scrape of claw and chisel against his gem-heart. The cage sways, shooting orange light flickering around the chest cavity while you cling to the wires. You manage to keep the chisel wedged in place beneath the cage, which, with the swaying, bends the wire further. As the wolf's convulsions subside, you wriggle the chisel until the orange gem-heart moves. A deep groan vibrates in your paws.

With one final push on the chisel, the wire snaps and the gem-heart pops free, clanging against the elysium chest. It glows an angry orange for a moment and then dims until you're sitting in near darkness.

The wolf collapses and you hang onto the damaged cage until everything settles. Then, using the light through the gaping chest plates, you retrieve the dark gem-heart and emerge from the wolf to find the shop full of damaged and shocked dragons.

"You're alive!" Blain rushes over and enfolds you in an awkward hug. When he steps back, you take in Marcus, who now bears a dent remarkably like Blain's. Beside him stands the Siren. One of her leather wings hangs limp against her red side. When it happened, you have no idea, but she holds herself proud. It's like the damage is a mark of her courage, which it is, you realize, as more and more dragons land or crawl onto the workbench.

Marcus steps toward you. For a moment you're tempted to bolt for the discard heap, but then you both look at the dead gem-heart clutched in your small paws.

"We all need some fixing, I guess," Marcus says.

It's the only apology he'll ever offer, and it's more than you ever expected he'd give.

"The Maker's got his work cut out for him," you agree finally.

You set the gem-heart in front of the wolf's motionless body, then plunk down in the middle of the workbench. Marcus actually chuckles as he and Blain join you.

"I can't wait to see the Maker's face when he walks in tomorrow morning," he says.

You and Blain laugh right along with everyone else in the shop as the tension drains away.

The End

Discarded Dragons

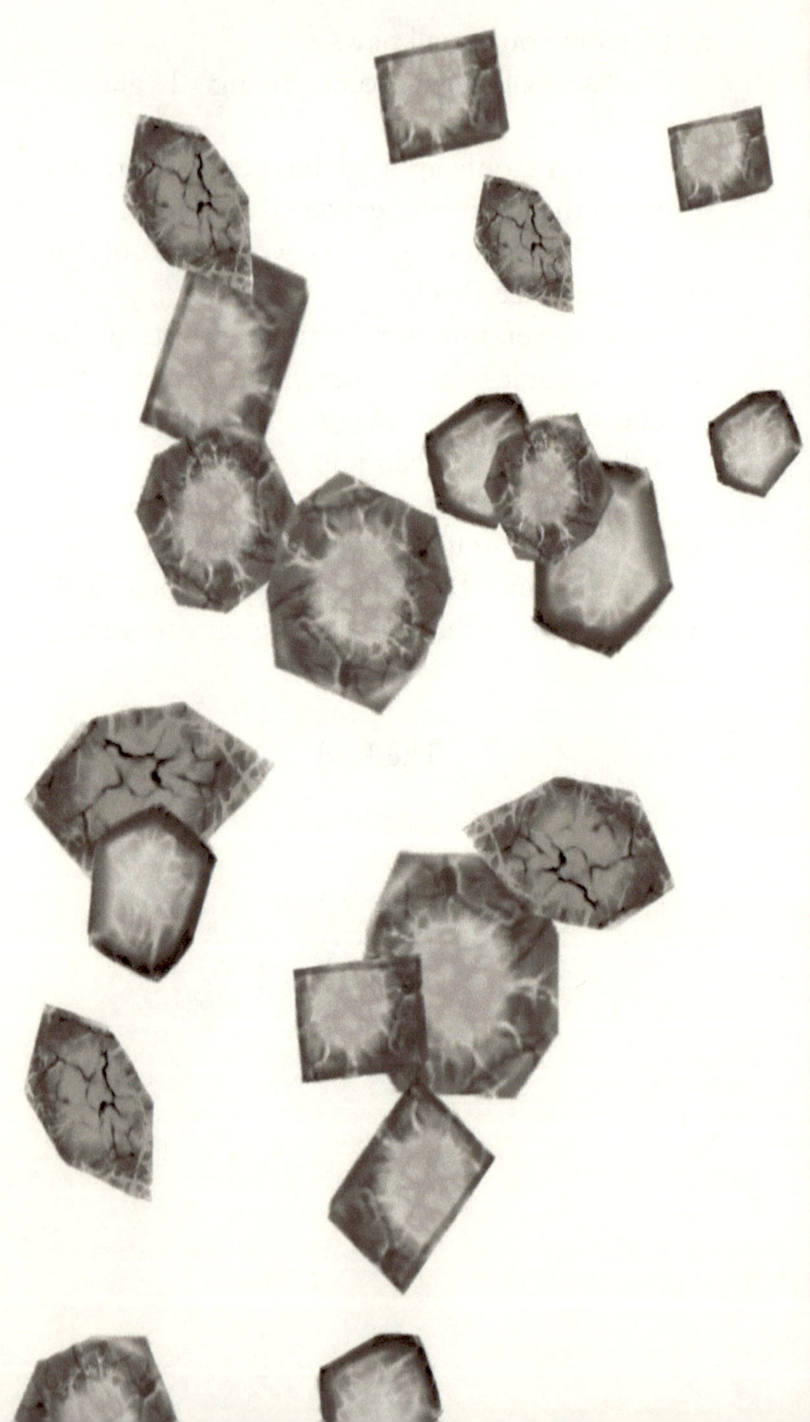

Gem-hearts are the only parts the Maker worries about keeping locked. He stores their box on a small shelf above the workbench but it's not so high that you can't reach it with a quick hop and flap of your wings.

You shove the metal box onto the bench below, where it clatters with the gem-hearts inside. On your way down to it, you grab a ball-peen hammer and a tiny chisel off the wall.

In the chaos, only Blain notices and he dodges his way over.

"What's the 'lan?" he asks.

"How's your aim with a hammer?" you ask in return.

"Good. Kind of good. As long as it's with my right 'aw."

"Good." You hand him the hammer. "Hit the chisel."

You fit the sharp point of the chisel into the box's lock and hold it steady for Blain to smash.

He looks at you, hammer held tight in his big claws. "I'll have to hit hard to break that," he says.

"Do it."

He winds back and slams the hammer against the butt end of the chisel. It hits dead on and the shock vibrates through the chisel, making your paws go numb. The lock cracks with a sharp screech.

Once the lid's flipped open, you stare at the treasure of gem-hearts inside. There are two compartments. One with dark gem-hearts waiting to be infused and one with glowing gem-hearts ready to be placed within new dragons.

You select a large turquoise one from the glowing pile. It's not the biggest, but you're not sure you can carry anything bigger.

"'Lan?" Blain asks again, glancing at the wolf, who's now got Marcus' chest plate peeled back. Inside glints a perfectly round amber gem the size of a grape. The dragon's squirming, fighting to prevent the wolf from sliding his large claws in to take his gem-heart.

You grab a pawful of the dull gems and slam the lid closed.

"Hide the box and find something to cover the skylight," you tell Blain.

His face falls. "I'll take the glowing heart," he says.

"You're strong, Blain, but not fast. Find something for the skylight."

He gulps, and nods agreement.

You take a couple steps toward the wolf and "trip." Dull gem-hearts tumble across the bench, some even pinging against Marcus' side and the wolf's paws. Both dragon and wolf look at you.

You don't have to feign terror when those glowing orange eyes settle on the bright turquoise treasure you hold. You clutch it to your chest and pivot to hide the gem from the wolf like you're trying to sneak away with it.

A grin pulls the metal around the wolf's jaws up with a creak. As you'd hoped, his expression lights with the joy of the chase.

You launch off the workbench, flapping your aluminum wings hard as you look up at the gaping hole where the skylight used to be. Your earlier fall didn't feel that far but now the distance only shrinks marginally with every flap of your wings.

You hear a growl from below, filled with dark joy. There's a thud and you can't help but glance down. The wolf swiped Marcus to the side where he tumbled off the bench and hit the floor. No longer interested in the downed dragon, the wolf stalks to a spot just below you and watches for a moment, letting you feel the terror of his glowing gaze.

The sight of Blain organizing a dozen dragons to pull a shelf off the wall galvanizes you. Just a little farther.

A thrill of triumph hits you as you give two more solid flaps and pass the torn window frame. Your right wing twinges with the strain.

Something seems loose near your shoulder blade but you keep flying.

Moments later, there's a scraping and a growl. It's then you know the wolf is toying with you. He jumped the distance from the workbench to the skylight, only needing a little assistance from his claws to pull himself the last bit through the hole in the roof. At any time, he could have caught you.

No matter, you reason, his toying made him leave the shop as you hoped.

You sail over the rooftop of the shop next to the Maker's and dart to the side to avoid a swiping paw. The wind of its passing hits your wing and pushes you farther than intended. You flare your wings to keep from spinning out of control and your right wing shudders oddly. You wobble but manage to keep from slamming into the roof.

Behind the wolf, a shelf appears through the window frame and dozens of dragon claws—some perfectly matching, some mismatched or bearing gaps—slide the plank to cover the gap. Only because you're listening for it do you hear the thudding of a hammer nailing the shelf into place.

Time to disappear.

You spin and pitch the turquoise gem-heart into the gaping jaws of the wolf. It catches in his throat and he coughs, spitting the gem back out, but it's enough of a distraction for you to dive into the alley.

You don't hear the wolf jumping after you. The only warning you get is the sudden gust of wind that hits your back moments before the wolf hits and drives you to the cobblestones. You try to flare your wings, maybe duck to the side, but the combined weight of the wolf and your body is too much. Your right wing rips free just before you thud into the ground.

Your head slams into the cobblestones with a metallic thud.

Blain peeks out the alley window that sits right above the dumpster the Maker uses. It took him hours to convince the other dragons to let him look outside, but finally they agreed as long as he keeps it quick. The latch on the window, a small pivot on the bottom, was easy for his big claws to push open.

Behind him dozens of dragons watch as he slides his head through the gap. Dawn barely brightens the alley in gray light. Other than the chunks of wood the wolf clawed from the roof the night before, there's no sign of the beast.

Blain slides his large body out the

window and drops to the edge of the dumpster.

"Hello?" he calls. "Are you there?"

There's no answer, so he wings down to the cobblestones.

"Hello," he calls again. Then he sees it. A single, thin, aluminum wing tucked just below the edge of the dumpster. His claws scrape against the cobblestones as he crouches to retrieve it.

The connection points are ripped and a large scratch folds the wing almost in two.

Blain shudders, sobbing while holding the wing to his chest, and returns to the shop just in time to close the window and dart into the discard heap before the Maker's key sounds in the lock. The other dragons are already settled on their shelves.

The Maker pauses at the mess he finds. He eyes the shelf covering the skylight and huffs. "Those constables better catch that beast soon," he mutters and starts to pick up, assessing each damaged dragon as he goes.

While he moves, dozens of eyes watch Blain. Finally, when the Maker's not looking, he holds up the mangled wing for them all to see. Eyes slowly dim and even the Siren bows her head. Blain clutches the wing close, waiting for night.

When he climbs up onto the bench that night, none of the dragons stop him. And when he places the wing onto the shelf where the

Maker keeps his prized keepsakes, they all bow their heads.

Then Blain heads for the drawer with the claws. He finds a couple for his front paws, but when he starts to search for his hind paws, he can't bend enough to reach the gap.

Marcus, who's on the bench for the Maker to fix the deep bend in his chest plate, climbs to his feet and wanders over.

Blain goes still.

"Here," the male holds out a paw, "let me help."

The End

You start moving before the half-finished female can react, digging your claws into the wood of the workbench for traction. A glance back reveals her opened mouth and its tiny points of teeth. You can see into the circle of her throat and realize the Maker has installed in her a siren's voice box. The cry that pierces the air freezes your limbs in shock.

Your momentum carries you forward even as your legs stutter and your run turns into an uncontrolled skid.

Not a dragon in the shop could have slept through that wail. As you hit the edge of the workbench, the rustle of wings and whir of gears skitters through the shop from several different locations.

The bench disappears from under you. The cry from the slender Siren fades and you regain motion in your body just in time to tuck into a roll. You hit the discard heap with a crunch of metal but the noise is lost in the renewed wail of the Siren.

Coming to rest amid the bits and pieces in the discard pile, you wriggle in deeper and go still only once a rusted cog and a cut spring cover part of your side like you've been in the heap longer than they have.

"Quiet!" a deep voice booms.

The Siren's wail is cut short.

"What is this racket?" asks the deep voice.

"There's a thief," answers the Siren. "One of the flawed things stole a gem."

Seeing where this is going, you quickly pop the green gem free of your eye socket and shove it into your mouth instead.

Through your murky glass eye, you see a long, many-plated tail the color of amber drape over the side of the workbench, twitching with irritation. There's the gentle clatter of gems being shuffled around in the jewel box.

"There's nothing missing," the male says.

"Because you know *all* the gems discarded into the box?" the Siren scoffs. "It stole a green gem and fell off the bench."

A moment later, the snout of a large amber dragon peeks over the side of the bench. He motions for two others to join him and the three fly down to the discard heap, the gust from their beautiful wings causing some of the smaller bits to tumble about. The dragons pick through the various unfinished or damaged dragons they find amidst the general scraps of metal, grimacing at the rust and creak of each part they touch.

The amber male reaches you and lifts you up to inspect your face.

You force your eye to go unfocused and dull, knowing you're no match for his powerful claws if he realizes you're aware. Finally, he huffs and tosses you over his shoulder to join the other Discards he's already inspected.

"There's no green gem down here," he announces after searching the top layer of the heap.

"I swear—"

"You received your sight today?" asks the male.

She huffs. "I know what I saw."

"Hmm," says one of the others. "Sight sick?"

"That'd be my guess." The male motions for them to return to the top of the workbench with him. "Sleep, new one," he encourages the Siren.

She huffs again but tucks her legs under her body.

The amber male hums while he and the others return to their shelves to relax into sleep again. It's a while before the slender Siren's ruby eyes dim. You hold the awkward position you fell in after the amber dragon tossed you aside, with one leg in the air and a thin wing crumpled under your body, until you can hear the deep breathing of her sleep.

Then you pop your green eye back in

and flip over to inspect the shop.

By chance, you were tossed toward the far side of the heap where it ends between the sales counter and the Maker's wall of parts, which includes his pairs of wings.

Now that you have a second eye, the next thing you need are wings. From where you stand, you can make out the individual wings where they hang by threads the Maker laces through their connection joints. Each hook holds three or four pairs. Not many of them are small enough for you, but upon closer inspection, you spot the glimmer of an aluminum pair two deep on the third hook in. The aluminum might be light enough for you to walk and move normally but strong enough to carry your weight in flight.

Your belly quivers with excitement but caution makes you glance around the shop. It's late now. Everyone's sleeping that deep sleep you fall into just before dawn. But there's not much time. If it's difficult to extract the wings from their hook, the Maker might walk in on you. If he sees you moving, he's likely to dismantle you as he has every dragon that's moved in front of him since one of them set his shop on fire.

Is there enough time to retrieve them tonight or do you wait?

If you seek new wings now, go to page 103
If you wait, go to page 135

You look at every dragon. Snores softly rumble from many of their snouts, including the Siren on the workbench.

Stepping with slow, quiet paws, you approach the wall and stare up at the hooks, planning your route to the aluminum wings winking at you from their spot. Your belly continues to quiver. The green eye was your first success in finishing your design and as you look at those wings, it finally seems possible that you'll succeed with the rest.

But first you have to climb up to that hook. Removing your current, useless wings would make the climb easier. You pivot to look at them, silently thanking the Maker for creating your torso with a series of overlapping plates so it's possible for you to turn far enough to see and touch the connections on your shoulder blades.

The thin wings are held on with a combination of wires and leather, but they're not hard to disengage from the machinations within your shoulders. In a moment, they fall free to the floor and you feel weightless as you approach the wall again.

Just as you climbed the drawer handles, you flip over to use your tail to reach

each row of hooks. If any of the dragons wake right now, they might die of laughter, calling you a salamander instead of a dragon, but you let that thought go. They laugh at you anyway for your incomplete frame; lacking wings and hanging upside down isn't going to make the situation worse. And soon, hopefully, you'll have wings that work.

You reach the row with the aluminum wings without clanking anything together. Laddering sideways, you grasp the desired hook and ever so slowly remove the set blocking the ones you want. They clink softly and you freeze, giving the shop a glance before proceeding.

The top set is heavier than you anticipated, so instead of holding them out of the way with your tail, you transfer them to the next hook over. It bows under the new weight, threatening to deposit its contents on the floor. You hold your breath as you let go. It bows further and then settles without going so far as to dump everything.

You sigh. With one reach, the aluminum wings are in your paws. They shine dully in the moonlight peeking through the skylight. Their interlocking plates are so perfectly fitted that they fold with the slightest pressure. Since their machinations are controlled through the wires sticking out of their connection joints, they fold neatly closed when you shove those wires into your mouth to hold them as you climb down. Just as you had to use your tail to get up, you have to use it to get down, which leaves your teeth for holding the wings. It's surprisingly easy with them folded in front of you.

The gray light of dawn is just starting to wash all color from the shop by the time your claws scrape against the floor. There's just enough time to attach the wings and get back to the discard heap.

Having removed your old wings, you recognize each wire and where it connects in your shoulders. You twine them carefully together, working on one thin wire at a time until you can pull on the single copper wire that pulls the wing into the slot of your shoulder blade and tightens everything down. As they fit into place and you tie them off, the awareness of their workings fills you like knowledge you've always had but finally understand. Giving the wings a slow flap or two, you wish you could cry.

"Huh," says a high, soft voice, "they actually fit you."

Terror freezes your gears like they're filled with ice until you finally convince your head to pivot toward the workbench. Above, the Siren peers down, a smirk on her face.

She grins and opens her jaws to screech a warning.

"They'll just think you're crazy," you say before that scream can shatter the silence. "I'll be back into the discard heap long before they come to investigate."

You wait for her to point out the flaw in your logic, that this time you wouldn't be able to hide the new wings from the amber dragon, but she only cocks her head with a huff.

"They're dumb," she says, and then a light enters her eyes. "Unlike you, I suppose. A new eye and wings all in one night! What an accomplishment. Let's see you fly with those wings. They must feel marvelous."

You flap them but otherwise don't move.

"No silly, fly. Show me how it's done for when I receive my own wings today. Let me see how they work. Mine are leather, but yours look like metal plates. Come, let me see them."

You recognize the light in her eyes because it mimics your own excitement to feel the wind below your wings. She must be bursting to try her own after the Maker installs them.

You ruffle your wings and the feel through your shoulder blades calls for you to use them. A short flight to the bench could be a great first test.

The dull gray from the skylight draws your eye. It'd be thrilling to peek out through that window just to see if you can reach that far. No one but the Siren is awake yet and you could savor the memory of your first flight while in the discard heap that day. But any flight is a risk as you're sure the Maker will arrive for work soon.

If you fly to the bench, go to page 109
If you fly to the skylight, go to page 117
If you refuse, go to page 129

Discar

You spread your glorious wings and for the first time in your life take a running leap into flight. The air presses close, pushing you higher in an exhilarating flash.

The Siren whoops softly and shares a grin with you.

She backs up as you wing your way into a spiral over the bench and then come in to land, a bit wobbly, onto the scarred wood.

"I can't wait," she says, and then flings a wire net over you.

The net is made to help hold a new dragon's pieces together while the Maker works. It snaps around the edges in a way that the Maker can hold a leg or a torso, depending on which snaps he connects. Some dragons are so complicated that the last screw is what pressure sets all their plates together and the net's the only way he's able to keep all the pieces in place before finishing.

Although it's a delicate net, it's strong. You try to flare your wings but find they only grate against the mesh. The Siren sneers as she snaps the ends together.

"It's a shame you got to experience flight before me," she says, "but I'll get to experience it a lot longer."

There's the click of a key in the back door of the shop. The Siren's grin vanishes and she drops the net to race to where the Maker left her the night before. Her eyes go dim just as the Maker flips on the lights.

If you had a second longer, you'd be able to wriggle free and jump into the discard heap, but now the Maker's setting his keys on the bench and his hand pauses as he notices you.

Terror makes your gem-heart quake. Never has a dragon attempted to finish their design after the Maker decided the parts weren't worth the effort. He's likely to dismantle you for your nerve.

The Maker's large hand unsnaps the net and absently hangs it back on the wall above the bench.

The Maker lifts your head between a calloused thumb and forefinger, inspecting your mismatched eyes. You think to dim your eyes, but a rebellious stubbornness within refuses. If he's going to dismantle you, let him know he's working on an aware dragon. In the light of the shop, his brows and nose look harsh through the grays and greens of your sight.

"That's odd," he mutters, picking you up.

It's the weirdest feeling when he extends your wings. You don't fight the movement, though.

"What gem-heart did I install in you?" he

wonders aloud. The next thing you know, he's unscrewing one of your chest plates. Terror truly clenches in your gem-heart now. A few movements and you're done if he decides to remove it.

"Mmmm." He creaks open the chest plate and clear light shimmers off his face. It's even weirder knowing you have a crystal gem-heart. Somehow, you've never considered the color of your heart before. After a moment of looking at your innards, the Maker closes your chest plate and replaces the tiny screw holding it in place. He taps the workbench in thought.

"Have to remember that," he says.

He turns, carrying you away from the bench over to the glass-sided Curiosity Box on the far wall of the shop.

A heady mix of emotions washes through you. Relief because the Maker apparently decided not to take you apart. Dread because the box is locked and you're not sure you can escape it. Then hope because if you're not dismantled but instead placed in the Curiosity Box, there's a chance for the future. Waiting for an opportune moment is something you know you can do.

The Maker unlocks the large box with a key from his vest pocket. Inside are all sorts of things that are just a little off.

There's a dragon with a droopy face. He was caught in the infamous shop fire but instead of his bindings burning away or his metal being singed, he melted. His face still moves. You've seen him trying to shout at night through the glass of the box, but he looks almost like the dough the baker gives to the Maker sometimes to take home.

You've seen the Maker use a propane torch to recreate the effect, giving some of his creations more bulbous bodies, but he keeps the melted dragon for a reminder.

Beside the melted dragon is a wing with multiple metals and a power-gem held in the cog at its base where the connection joint usually sticks out. The Maker tried to connect the wing with a gem instead of wires and leather. The gem overpowered the wing like a lightning strike and all the screws became welded to the plates, freezing it into an open position. The Maker still attempts to make a gem-powered wing, but he's more cautious with the metals he uses. He hasn't figured out a way to make it work yet.

The last thing you see as he sets you into the box is a long, sinuous dragon without wings. From what you understand, someone told the Maker about a different kind of flesh dragon from the East. He decided to craft one from the stories but no one wanted it because it was unfamiliar.

Its smooth, many-plated green body looks like it could wrap around you three or four times, but it's a beautiful beast and you see a glimmer, almost like a wink, as the top of the box closes and the Maker locks you inside.

The long Eastern dragon's head rises as the shop lights go out. A moment later, you see his deep green eyes glow as he awakens and stares at you.

Beside him, the melted dragon's eyes also awaken, coming alight with a clear amethyst glow.

"Hello?" you say.

"Oh, hello! I say, you make for good sport. We were betting on your wing heist last night and old Rufus won." The melted beast grins.

"It was a safe bet," Rufus, the Eastern dragon, says in a smooth bass voice. "After all, the eye-gem was harder to retrieve than the wings."

"But it was so late. Surely there wasn't enough time!"

"Clearly there was." Rufus winks at you.

"Would you two pipe down," says a voice on the far side of Rufus. A tiny female dragon you hadn't noticed before flutters over Rufus and lands in front of you. She's so small that she could fit in the palm of your paw. "Welcome to the Curiosities, dear," she says. Noticing your amazed stare, she places a tiny, pale blue paw on your leg. "The Maker used tweezers, dear, to fit my parts together. Took him almost a month." A proud gleam enters her sapphire eyes. "I'm one of a kind. Like you! Now, I assume you'll want to get free. I bet *you'll* succeed—at some point."

"I'll take that bet," the melted dragon says. "We've been trying to get out for forever!"

"Yes, dear, but we never stole wings or eyes, either."

You smile as they banter. Even if it takes you *forever* as the melted dragon thinks, at least it won't be a boring wait. Your only regret is the box isn't large enough for you to fly. But that just gives you more incentive to escape. Like he can read your thoughts, Rufus winks at you again before taking the bet.

The End

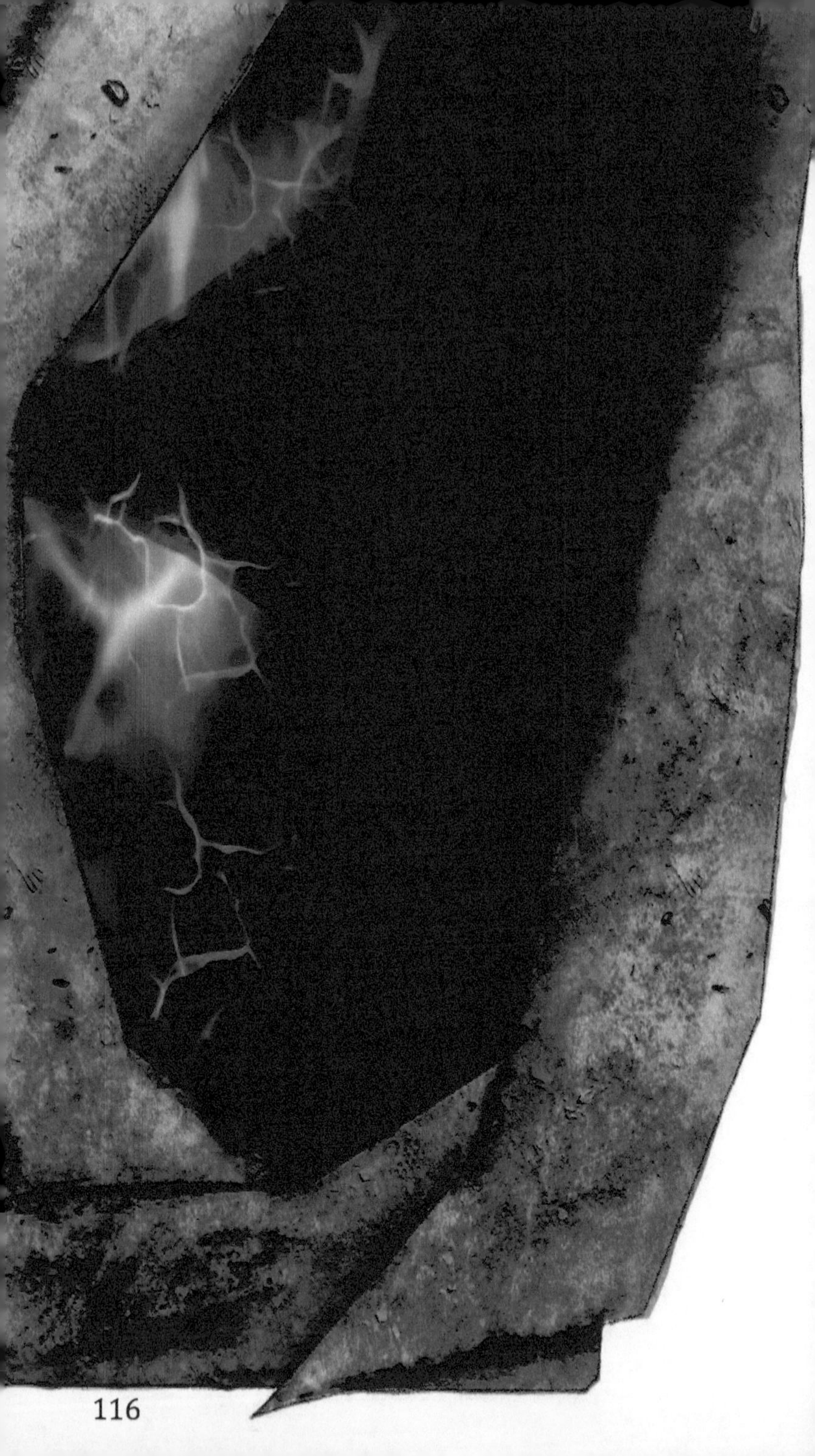

You spread your glorious wings and, for the first time in your life, take a running leap and fly. Your wings catch the air in an exhilarating flash of smooth movement and wind.

The Siren whoops softly and shares a grin with you but her expression falls when you pass the bench and wing for the gray dawn light showing through the skylight above.

A thrill fills your chest. You're airborne! The gentle swish of dusty air moving past you feels like a caress, welcoming you to the sky.

There's a rattling, clanking thud from below and a cry of indignation from the slender Siren. You hear the beat of much bigger wings and look down in alarm.

But instead of a Perfect dropping off a shelf to attack, there's a large gray beast emerging from the discard heap. He bears a dent down his left side and gaps between his claws. But his wings, which are made from solid pieces of metal instead of folding plates, eat up the distance between you.

The Siren throws a cracked gem at the beast. It pings off his side but doesn't seem to register on the excited grin on his face. He swoops past you, stalls purposefully just below the skylight, and then spins into a dive that gusts air against your wings with his passing.

You ride the gust, using it to reach higher, and peak in flight just like he did, staring at the fire of dawn through the skylight for the brief moment you stall just before diving.

He chuckles as you soar past the bench together and land near the discard heap.

"I a' Blain," the other Discard introduces himself, distorting "am" slightly due to the dent in the left side of his face. "That was the best night ever! Can we do it again?"

You're about to answer when a key rattles in the back door of the shop. The door opens and Blain goes limp beside the heap.

You're farther away than he is, closer to the front of the sales counter than the heap, but there's no time to dart for safety. You go limp, hoping the Maker doesn't wander around the front of the counter for the day.

You feel the Maker's steps through the wood of the floor as he enters, flips on the lights, and hangs up his jacket.

"I've got a wonderful selection," he says

as he moves to the bench.

The floor vibrates with footsteps until a young girl and her father move into your line of sight. As they approach, Blain cocks his head toward the sales counter.

"Fly," he whispers, staring at the low shelf along the front of the counter where the Maker displays his smallest dragons. There's an empty spot there, right at the young girl's eye level.

You check once, just to make sure no one's watching, then push to your feet and with two awkward steps and a strong flap of your wings, you glide into that empty spot.

The girl turns, her eyes intent as she takes in the shelf of small dragons. Her narrow fingers trace the lines in a blue dragon's snout, then gently follow the arc of a water dragon's flared wing, and continue on to the points of the next dragon's exposed teeth. As she draws near, you smell the faint hint of glue just like the kind the Maker uses, along with the undertones of brass on her fingers when she curiously touches the end of your stunted tail.

She notices your mismatched glass and jasper eyes, frowning.

In a flash of sudden courage, you wink.

She gasps, but after a moment of staring, she grins. "This one, Papa," she points.

Her papa steps over from speaking with the Maker and kneels down to look. He's a big man with a red beard that makes it hard to read his expression.

"That dragon's broken, Eira." He shakes his head and starts to stand.

"I'm okay with that, Papa," she says.

He looks back at you and you're tempted to wink again, except even your first small wink had been a huge risk. The Maker tends to dismantle dragons who move in front of customers. He likes his shop orderly and quiet.

You could be more respectful and bow to the big man. That might not be quite so bold as winking but still catch his attention.

The girl's papa frowns as he inspects you. If they leave without buying you, you're sure the Perfects will make you pay for your daring, but you're not sure what's worse, chancing the Maker dismantling you or the Perfects' retribution.

If you wink again, go to page 53
If you stay still, go to page 77
If you bow, go to page 123

Jennifer M Zeiger

You've already chanced the Maker's wrath, you figure. And Blain's encouraging you by repeatedly winking from where he lays on the floor. A small bow shouldn't harm your chances much. Your nerves make you shaky as you bend your legs and bow.

The big man's just turning away and catches the motion out of the corner of his eye, but unfortunately your nerves turn the bow from jittery into wobbly. You flare your wings to balance, but the motion is unfamiliar and you hit the dragons on either side of you.

Their eyes flash as they topple sideways. They maintain their stiff postures, so they simply land on their sides. You straighten and take a step, trying to regain your balance, but the side of your paw hits the edge of the shelf and—half trying to remain still, half trying to save yourself—you topple to the floor with a metallic thud.

"What?" The Maker's footsteps vibrate through the floor and into your metal body where you lay on the wood.

The three humans stare down until the girl's papa says, "I'm sorry, Eira, but I don't know about that one."

She sighs but must recognize the stern expression on his face because she doesn't complain when he points to the green dragon you tipped over.

"How about this one?"

She picks it up, seeming more interested in the scratch your wing left in the dragon's side than with the dragon itself. She agrees and they buy the dragon.

The Maker's callused fingers curl around you and he carries you to the bench before finishing the sale.

As you stare at the angry eyes of the red Siren on the bench with you, disappointment wells in your chest. You were so close! But now the Maker's likely to dismantle you for moving in front of a customer. It's hard to be still as the Maker returns to the bench after his customers leave.

He picks you up again and inspects your aluminum wings, then your eyes, then your stubby tail. He reaches for a pair of pliers hanging on the wall and you want to cry, but then he pulls open a drawer and withdraws a set of graduated metal rings. Setting you back on the bench, he tries several on the end of your tail until he finds the next size down and bends the metal into place. And on he works, finishing your tail as the Siren's eyes burn while she watches.

"He can't possibly mean to finish you!" the Siren wails.

A Perfect snorts from his spot on a shelf. "He wouldn't add metal to a dragon he doesn't intend to finish. Now simmer down and go to sleep."

The Siren huffs and curls up. "You're lucky," she grumbles. "He should've dismantled you."

"I know," you admit. "But the girl showed interest in buying me; maybe he figures I'll sell."

She scoffs. "No one will buy you over me."

You don't argue, but you also don't agree as you settle in to sleep after giving Blain a wink over the side of the bench.

The Maker finishes you by giving you another green eye-gem in place of the glass one. The world lights up in clear shades of emerald, aqua, and jasper.

You're still marveling at the beauty of the shop through your matching eyes when the Maker finishes the aggravated Siren and sets her on the shelf beside you.

When he's not looking, you grin at her and she scowls back, but then the Maker turns and affixes a string around both your necks with a small slip of paper.

"A matching set," he says, taking you in as a pair and nodding.

When he turns away, the Siren says out of the side of her mouth, "There's no way I'm a matching set with you."

It's not ideal, you agree, but then, you're a finished dragon and who knows what the day may bring.

"Hush," you say. "It's only temporary."

She huffs but settles. You imagine this is what it's like to have a temperamental sibling. With a huff of your own, you settle as well.

The End

You smile knowingly and shake your claw at the clever Siren.

"I've already cut this night close," you say. "It's high time for me to disappear." You flap and hop to the heap while she leans farther over the edge of the bench to keep you in sight.

"Oh, come on, that's barely enough to see if the wings will work. A quick flight won't hurt anything! It's got to be killing you not to test those wings in true flight."

You *do* want to give the wings a try. Even with your short hop, you felt the uplift of wind under the folding metal plates and the glorious pressure against your shoulder blades.

The Siren opens her mouth to say more but before she can speak, a key rattles in the lock of the back door. She bolts for her position on the bench and you wiggle down into the heap just as the Maker turns on the lights.

By the time he turns around, you have a ripped piece of leather and a bent cog covering your back, obscuring your beautiful new wings from the Maker's sharp gaze. He hums through the day and you plan the coming night.

If you finish your tail, all of the parts that affect your balance will be complete, so you stare at the drawer with the thin metal rings you need. It's halfway up the face of the bench.

You'll have to use the handles of the other drawers to help steady yourself—you negate that thought—you now have wings to help you pull the drawer open.

A smile pulls up the corners of your lips but the slight creaking this makes is lost under the thud of the Maker's steps as he moves about the shop.

Finally, twilight darkens the shop windows and the Maker carefully puts everything away for the night. New wings grace the magnificent Siren's back but she's bound in a clamp to help them dry. The Maker fixed them in place, making them stronger, with a flexible glue that requires a full day to set.

This makes you smile again. She won't be bothering you tonight.

The Maker pauses for a moment and sniffs, perhaps realizing how heavy the glue smell is in the shop. He hauls over a chair to stand on and grabs a broom. Then he pushes the skylight up and open with the handle before he finally turns off the lights and leaves, locking the door behind him.

You wait, as usual, for the other dragons to drift off. After a short time, their familiar snores fill the quiet. With a shake, you free yourself of the heap and approach the bench.

Then you remember you don't have to climb the handles tonight. You back up, eager to fly. This tilts you off balance since you're not used to the aluminum weight of your wings. You steady yourself with a couple steps, and then take flight to reach the drawer you desire.

The flap of your wings makes a soft whoop in the quiet shop. One, two, three, and you're at the drawer. You grasp the handle in your claws and pull. The drawer sticks and then slides free with a screech.

You look around and then duck into the drawer, nervous the noise might have woken another dragon.

"I know you're down there," says the high-voiced Siren.

You don't answer, still peeking out of the drawer at the other dragons in the shop.

"Come now, at least talk to me or I'll scream and you'll have dragons all over you."

Other than her voice, nothing in the shop moves or makes a sound. Stretching your neck, you peer over the top of the workbench to spot the Siren in the Maker's clamp.

"They'll just think you're crazy," you say and then duck back into the drawer, finding links to finish your tail. The Maker would use a pair of pliers to bend the links together with the others, but you find your claws strong enough to connect the links without tools.

The moon shines straight down into the shop by the time your tail is complete. It bears a number of dents and curves the Maker would never have been satisfied with, but to you it feels like you could spin in circles on the spot without tumbling.

Climbing out of the drawer, you grip the edge of it with your claws, spread your wings, and take flight. Above, the moon beckons you toward the skylight. The feeling of strength, of sinuous movement, and the power to climb mere air rushes through you and, before you know it, you're at the skylight and warm night air gently presses against your face through the gap.

When you glance below, the Siren's ruby eyes glitter, watching, but you find there's nothing to draw you back into the shop. Sure, you still have small pieces you could fix, but compared to your eye, wings, and tail, they're unimportant.

And that wind smells of adventure and new things, of a life you never thought you could grasp. With one last look over your shoulder, you wing through the gap in the skylight to explore the wide world.

The End

Although the thrill of success feels like uncontrollable energy driving you to move, you also don't want to fall off the wall because you're rushing to find new wings.

With a sigh that rattles in your chest, you return to a deeper section of the discard heap and wriggle your way beneath a few layers. Then you settle in, letting your limbs go slack as you calm yourself to go to sleep.

Just as you're about to drift off, there's a vibration in the metal. Flakes of rust shudder off a shoulder plate and land on your nose.

You shift, hiding your green eye against a piece of leather, and watch through your glass eye, expecting to find the amber male or the Siren come to look further. But it's neither of the Perfects who lift the shoulder plate above you. It's a huge gray dragon with a dent running the left side of his head. His golden-yellow eyes sparkle as he sees you're awake.

"'Ay I join you?" he asks, the dent in his face distorting "may" into "'ay."

This is new. Although you've always been aware that some of the other Discards are conscious, none of them have ever tried to speak with you before. Admittedly, you never thought of speaking to them either.

"Sure?" you say, questioningly.

The iron dragon wriggles his way in

beside you, not noticing the question in your answer. Once he's settled with his large, unfolding wing overtop your back, he lowers his chin to rest on his paws and grins.

"That was great!" he whispers.

"What?"

"You 'aking all the 'Erfects, especially the a'ber one, 'Arcus, think the new red dragon's sight sick. Brilliant!"

"More luck than anything," you say, realizing his speech distortion turned the amber dragon, Marcus, into 'Arcus.

"'Blain couldn't do it."

"Blain?"

He grins even bigger. "Yes?"

It dawns on you he was referring to himself. "You're Blain?"

"Yeah. What are you planning next?"

You hesitate. What if one of the Perfects overhears? But then you shake your head, negating the thought. They're sleeping and you doubt they can hear your whispering even if they weren't.

"Wings," you answer.

"'Ay I join you?"

At first you open your mouth to say no but then you look at the wall and realize

Blain's help might be just what you need to succeed.

"Sure," you say, "but we need to wait until tomorrow night. Maybe the night after."

Continue on page 139…

Blain twitches and something shifts in the discard heap. You can't see it from where you lay, half buried to hide from the Maker and the Perfects, but you hear the slither of something on leather and then a metallic thud as it hits the wooden floor.

Blain cringes without you hushing him again. You told him you're going to wait for at least one more night since all the Perfects, especially the irritable Siren, are on edge. He didn't argue. In fact, he nodded like you'd just given him the sagest advice he'd ever heard, but keeping his excitement in check is a challenge and you wonder what another night of inactivity will do to him.

The Maker turns an eye to the discard heap, frowning, but when nothing else moves, he goes back to adding links to the Siren's tail.

It's a relief when the Maker starts putting tools away for the day. Although you're not going to attempt anything during the night, at least any sounds Blain accidentally makes shouldn't draw too much attention unless you leave the heap.

Finally, the Maker shrugs into his jacket and turns off the lights. The door clicks and you hear the turn of his key before the shop goes still.

Something shudders in the heap and

there's a ponderous clang.

"Blain!" you admonish.

"It wasn't 'e!"

"Sorry," a third voice squeaks.

Blain and you peek out of the heap, craning to place the voice. A thin, three-legged dragon climbs out from under a ratty swatch of leather and hobbles his way to you by using his long, slender wing to compensate for the lack of a right front leg. Once he reaches you, he settles in against Blain's far side, using Blain's much larger wing to shield him.

Blain can't quite turn to see the creature since it's against his dented side, but his golden-yellow eyes go almost cross-eyed as he tries to look.

"Name's Eddy. Heard something about finding wings," the thin dragon says. "Can you help me fashion a leg while you're at it? I can't quite figure out how to create one myself with only one front leg."

Over the course of the night, a dozen more discarded dragons find their way to your spot in the heap. It's overwhelming. With so many moving about the shop at night, you're sure it'll be impossible not to alert the Perfects, but you also can't find the heart to tell them no.

At first you suggest focusing on only one part for one dragon at a time and, although they like the idea, it quickly turns into a debate about who gets parts first. Their voices grow so loud you have to hush them when several Perfects perk up at the noise. You all hunker down and wait for the next couple of hours until the glowing eyes dim.

"All right," you finally say. "We'll pair up in teams of two and find parts that way. Each team will get an hour a night. That way we'll hopefully not make too much noise."

Blain grins and nods, the slender dragon, Eddy, follows his lead, and none of the others object. You dole out the teams and settle in to wait for the next night's heist.

Blain, your partner, quivers in excitement while you both watch three-legged Eddy and his partner, a round female missing her wings named Maria, work their way up the face of the bench to the drawers with the metal links and cogs for legs. They're the first of the night and they're moving well together. A spark of hope ignites in you that this might actually work.

Maria reaches for the next drawer handle. She grasps it easily but when she puts her weight on it, it shifts in her claws. She gives a delicate gasp.

The sound is so soft, it shouldn't have

alerted anyone, but instantly the Siren's slender head peeks over the edge of the bench.

"I knew it," she exclaims. And then she lets out a wail that hits Eddy and Maria like a wave and knocks them clean off the front of the bench. They hit the floor in a mess of limbs but can't move until the Siren runs out of breath.

By then, three Perfects have already left their shelf. They dive for the two hapless Discards and hit them just as the Siren goes quiet. Claws tear into sides and wings and Eddy screams a thready, copper cry.

Without thinking or coordinating, you're out of the discard heap and leaping onto the back of the large amber male who Blain called Marcus.

Blain's not far behind, but before he can help hold Marcus to the ground, the amber dragon flares his multi-plated wings and takes flight with you on his back. You sink your claws into the plates lining his spine. With great heaves, Marcus climbs higher and higher until you realize he's carrying you toward a shelf where a couple more Perfects wait to tear you from his back.

You can't face three Perfects, especially this high off the ground, and expect to win. Making a flash decision, you let go and roll off his back with the next down sweep of his wings. As you hoped, he's just passing the

Maker's Curiosity Box of unusual dragons and parts where it sits on its own shelf.

You land on the glass top and slide before you dig your claws into the frame to keep from going over the edge. Your thin wings won't carry you but you flare them and it's enough to regain your balance.

A glance above warns you just as Marcus turns and dives with his long claws reaching. You heave yourself fully onto the box and roll. His claws hit the frame where you were a second before and dig in, tearing chunks from the wood before he swoops away for a second dive. You can't help but peek at the damage he did.

His claws left gouges in the wood and broke the lock that held the lid of the Curiosity Box closed.

This sparks an idea—if you climb over the edge and lift the lid just as Marcus dives again, you might be able to close the lid on top of him.

You're about to crawl over the side to do just that when your eye catches on a flash of red and gray below. The Siren's wail registers on your distracted brain, but it's Blain you stare at. He's pinned to the floor by the Siren's scream and she's approaching him with what looks like one of the Maker's sharp chisels.

If you trap Marcus, will it stop the others? He seems to lead them, but the Siren looks narrowly focused on Blain. Will she even realize it if you capture Marcus?

You could jump onto Marcus as he dives and use him as a step to reach the bench. From there you know you can safely jump to reach Blain.

If you try to capture Marcus, go to page 147
If you help Blain, go to page 153

Jennifer M Zeiger

You hang from the side of the Curiosity Box like you're trying to figure out how to get down. It's not hard to look like you're desperate because, as Marcus peaks in his flight and spins to dive again, your paws start to shake where you have them braced on the frame of the box.

You hold in your mouth the remains of the lock that you slid free a moment before. You'll need it if you manage to trap Marcus inside the glass. The padlock's broken, but once you slide it back through the slotted latch, that won't matter for the amber dragon trapped inside.

You shoot a look over your shoulder and give a tinny, "Eeek." Marcus is almost on top of you.

You heave, feinting upward like you're trying to scurry on top and out of his way. Marcus adjusts to hit you higher, and at the last second, you shove the lid open instead of climbing onto it. This leaves you still hanging onto the lip of the box while the lid smacks into the shop wall.

Unable to adjust again, Marcus thuds into the underside of the lid and tumbles into the glass box. You lunge, grasping the lid again and shoving off the wall to close the box but long amber claws sneak out right as it's slamming closed.

The impact shears off two claws. The roar from inside rattles the glass beneath your feet and the remaining claws pull away. The box snaps shut with the slotted latch falling over the ring meant for the lock hanging from your mouth.

You scramble, sliding the broken lock through the ring just as Marcus crashes into the lid from below. It shudders and, although you've never heard a peep from the other occupants of the box before, you still hear the dragon's roar as he backs up again, and again, and again, trying to open the lid.

Every time he hits the glass, it shudders under your paws and slides the box forward on the shelf. After a third, then a fourth, and a fifth collision, the box tilts and you race to the back edge to keep the whole thing from teetering off its shelf. The occupants inside do so as well and one, a long sinuous dragon styled after an Eastern flesh dragon, has the courage to wrap his long body around Marcus until he can't ram into the lid again.

It's obviously a strain to hold him, but the Eastern dragon clamps tight until Marcus subsides.

It's then you realize the entire shop sits

silent. Every dragon watches, some from below, some on their shelves, and some in the air.

That silence holds for a moment, held by disbelief and something akin to terror.

Then a roar, a deep, metallic roar of triumph, rattles the windows of the shop and you realize it's coming from Blain. The other Discards join him and the Perfects shy from the primal sound.

"We're allowed to find parts," you repeat.

The three Perfects on the bench cringe, but nod.

"And you won't attack."

They nod again.

Marcus still sits in the Curiosity Box. It's securely on its shelf again, pushed back into place by Blain and a few others, but you're unwilling to free the amber dragon until negotiations are done. His glowering eyes are a poignant reminder to the Perfects that fighting can go just as poorly for them as it can for you. Even a number of the free Perfects bear ugly scratches and dents that would, technically, send them to the discard pile if the Maker noticed them.

"And we're allowed to repair our own," one of the Perfects says.

You find it interesting that, although a large number of them are now damaged, they still rank among the Perfects. You would not have expected that loyalty among them.

"And you're allowed to repair your own," you agree.

The Maker rummages around in his drawer of cogs, looking for the right size to finish a new dragon's leg.

He mutters, "I could've sworn I had four…"

You glance up at the shelf that lines the ceiling. On it, a Perfect slides backward, hiding his hind leg that now bears a new cog, a replacement for the one that broke off during the fight. It's not the first part that's gone missing on the Maker, nor will it be the last.

You share a small grin with Blain, who sits beside you admiring his new claws.

The End

Jennifer M Zeiger

You can't tear your eyes from Blain. He's flattened to the floor by the Siren's powerful scream. He struggles to get his paws over his ears, but he looks like a marionette with slipping strings. Each small movement is accompanied by an involuntary flattening to the ground a moment later.

A whoosh warns you of Marcus diving. You back up against the wall and race toward the other dragon. As soon as he's close enough, you lunge.

He dodges and your claws catch on his hind paw instead of digging into his back like you'd hoped. He sinks with your sudden weight. It's just enough for you to swing and launch yourself toward the benchtop.

Limbs cartwheeling, you sail through the air. The thud you make as you slam into the scarred wood of the bench is lost in the chaos. Rolling, you hit the back of the bench, knocking several tools off the wall. Instantly, you're on your feet, careening toward the edge above where the Siren has Blain flattened. You can still hear her scream.

Without looking, you dive off the bench. You realize immediately that your aim's off. Instead of being above Blain, you fall toward the Siren. Perhaps the error's a good one, you think midfall, because this way you won't land in front of her scream.

You hit the back of the slender red dragon and there's a *crack* that you hear *and* feel. Except you don't experience any pain.

Rolling away, you turn to look at the slender Siren. She's silent. Stunned.

You landed on her new leather wings. The delicate metal frame on both sides snapped near her body. Now both wings drape down her sides like a leather cape split down the middle. As the shock subsides, she turns to you and opens her mouth.

A large paw clamps her jaws shut. Blain clicks his tongue and shakes his head in a wordless "no."

This gives you a second or two to take in the overall battle and you see immediately that the Discards are not faring well. It's time to retreat and take a measure of the damages.

"Take her to the heap," you tell Blain, and then you shout, "Retreat!"

Moments later discarded dragons are diving into the heap, splaying parts and rust in all directions until every dragon is buried in the debris.

An impasse ensues. Perfects continue to fly through the shop, waiting for someone to emerge while you, in turn, wait for them to get bold enough to dig through the heap. Seconds, then minutes, tick by until you realize that none of the Perfects are willing to sully themselves in actually pawing through the pile.

"Think we're safe?" Blain asks in your ear. He's got the petulant Siren tucked against his side with a paw still holding her mouth shut.

"For now," you say.

Beside him, the Siren's limp, the fight gone from her ruby eyes.

"You can probably let her go now," you say.

"You sure?"

"She could run from the heap." You shrug. "But with those broken wings, the Perfects are as likely to view her as a Discard as they are to help her."

Blain lets go and she flops, whimpering. Then some of the defiance returns to her gem-eyes.

"You're good at this," she says. "Help me fix my wings."

"Why should we?" Blain asks before you have the chance.

"You're the ones who broke them," she shoots back.

"I seem to remember someone with a chisel and a scream," you say.

She scoffs. "*You're* the ones stealing."

"To fix your wings, *you'll* have to steal parts too or use discarded parts."

She huffs. You've never met a dragon so prone to drama.

For the next several days, while you and the Discards recover as best you can using parts in the heap, the Siren hides and glares at anyone who comes too close.

You're almost asleep on the third night after the battle when you feel something shift in the heap and you open your eyes to see two glowing rubies.

"What?" you ask.

"I'll make a deal with you," the Siren says. "Help me fix my wings and I'll negotiate a peace with the Perfects."

A part of you wants to simply tell her no. But the idea of being able to wander the shop, free to find parts without the worry of attack, is attractive. Although most of the Discards have managed to repair themselves from random parts in the heap, it's a limping success. Wings and legs are still missing. One dragon lost an eye and you know how frustrating that is.

But do you trust the clever Siren to hold up her end of the deal? She's staring at you, waiting for your answer.

____

If you refuse the deal, go to page 159
If you make the deal, go to page 165

While you think about the Siren's offer, her eyes gleam, both cunning and disgust edging her expression. If she could repair her wings without help, she'd be more than willing to flatten you where you lay in the discard heap.

Therein lies the crux of your problem. The Perfects won't even listen to her until her wings are made whole again, but as soon as she gets what she wants, she's just as likely to leave you stranded as she is to help you negotiate.

It's circular and leaves you counting on her good graces.

"I don't trust you to hold up your end of the deal," you tell her honestly. "Fix your wings yourself."

Her face contorts in rage and she screeches so loud the heap shudders. Feeling it, the Siren cowers as the sound takes on a life of its own, waking Perfects and Discards alike.

Marcus shakes, stands up on his shelf, and glowers at the heap. Others follow his example and he lets out a roar before diving off the shelf.

"Look what you made me do!" the Siren cries, diving deeper into the heap.

Blain just shakes his head as he passes her in a rush to join you. In his large claws is a solid steel chest plate that looks warped from some sort of heat.

He holds it in front of you both as a shield.

Peeking around it, you spot Marcus in time to throw your shoulder against the back of the steel, helping Blain take the impact of the amber dragon's claws.

They screech across the metal and then he wings away, only to be replaced by another dragon who hits the steel and tries to rip it from Blain's claws. Blain clamps down and hangs on, sinking his gapped claws into the edge of the steel.

Eddy, even with his missing front leg, appears at your other side, awkwardly pulling his own chunk of metal.

"You're all brilliant," you exclaim and start searching the discard heap. Finally, you spot a long shaft, the remnants from a spine. It's snipped because it was longer than the Maker needed, but it's long enough to serve your purpose.

Grasping it in your paws, you rejoin Blain and Eddy and explain what you want them to do. Then you wait until Marcus dives again.

At the last moment before he hits their shields, they part a fraction of an inch, just enough for you to thrust the long metal spine between and catch the dragon on his shoulder. It pierces between the metal joints with a grating creak.

The force of his dive drives you back until he hits the edges of the shields. When he stalls, you pull the spine free of his joint. There's a deep growl, pain and anger mixed, as he wings away again with his front leg hanging limp instead of tucking in close to his chest.

Blain and Eddy cheer and reset for the next diving dragon.

Around you, other Discards have set up similar teams, holding ground against the aerial attack.

Only when the gray of dawn lightens the shop does the battle abate.

High above on his shelf, Marcus holds himself in an awkward position and you realize he's trying to hide the front leg that's not responding.

He should have just lain down, you realize, as the Maker enters the shop and pauses, scanning the shelves and floor and bench with his brows furrowed.

Parts from the discard heap lay scattered about the floor. Many Perfects sit or stand in unfamiliar positions, either favoring a hurt limb or trying to hide aesthetic damage. And you suppose, if you were seeing the heap from above, you might notice the large chunks of metal rimming it in a circle almost like a wall.

The Maker huffs, and then begins looking at every single dragon on his shelves. He gathers any into his hands that show damage, including Marcus, and heads for a window at the back of the shop.

You and Blain share a startled look. The Maker opens the window where it swings from its top hinges, and pitches the damaged dragons out. The window swings shut but not before you hear the clanking thud of metal hitting metal, of dragons hitting the dumpster.

Then the Maker heads for the discard heap where you and Blain lay. You hold onto each other's paws as he picks you up and adds you to the growing heap in the dumpster. As soon as you hit the debris, you both move to the edge and hang onto the rim, knowing full well what it's like to be buried in debris.

Since the Maker spends the rest of the day clearing the refuse off his floor, making trip after trip to the back window until you're sure the floor is clean for the first time in years, you end up surrounded by broken dragons and parts, but at least you're not buried.

Then the window thuds shut and clicks as the lock is engaged.

It's long moments before anyone moves. Then, the rustling begins as each dragon struggles to free itself from the mass of junk metal and leather and cracked jewels surrounding you.

With each dragon that emerges, the angry glares intensify between Discards and former

Perfects. When Marcus finally surfaces, you and Blain and the other Discards are already braced to defend yourselves.

The simmering anger in the dragon's jasper eyes makes your paws shake around the long spear-like piece you hold to protect yourself. Marcus grabs his own weapon in his one good front paw and is about to charge when there's a sound.

"Take a look!" says a young voice.

The disheveled, dirt-covered heads of two boys appear as they peer over the edge of the dumpster. At first excitement hits you—the possibility that these humans might take you home—but then they start pawing through the debris, tearing everything apart that they find without regard for what it is. One of them reaches for a red tail amidst the metal rubbish.

It twitches away and the boy yells, "Hey!" and starts digging for the Siren with glee lighting his eyes.

You share a look with Blain, then with Marcus, and then you all turn to defend yourselves against this new danger.

The End

While you think about the offer, the Siren's eyes gleam, both cunning and disgust edging her expression. If she could repair her wings without your help, she'd be more than willing to flatten you where you lay in the discard heap.

Therein lies the crux of your problem. The Perfects won't even listen to her until her wings are made whole again, but as soon as she gets what she wants, she's just as likely to leave you stranded as she is to help you negotiate.

"Why should I trust you to hold up your end of the deal?" you finally ask.

She huffs. "Because I said I would."

"Not good enough," you say.

Again she huffs, but she sits back on her haunches to think. She sits like that for so long that you're about to drift off again when she pushes on your forehead.

"What?" you ask, sleep clogging your throat.

"What if I let you remove the flight tendons from inside my wings? They'll look normal, I'll be able to move them, but they won't support flight. The Perfects won't know and you have your guarantee." She's so pleased with her idea that she's grinning with all her tiny, sharp teeth showing.

Blain hums from where he lays beside

you. "It's not a bad idea if she can 'ake a deal with the 'Erfects. 'Aybe we can actually get 'arts for all of us. We're all in bad shape."

The Siren's grin widens even more.

"Hello?" The Siren calls from the middle of the shop floor.

It took two full nights of everyone scrounging in the discard heap to find the right colored parts for her leather wings; you couldn't just use any old part. She had to look like a Perfect, not just function like one.

All the while, you couldn't emerge from the heap to look for new parts while the Perfects were watching. They reacted to even your small rummaging sounds. Marcus in particular circled overhead most of each night. But eventually, your effort of scrounging paid off and the heap yielded the needed parts.

Now the Siren's wings drape over her sides in graceful arcs, cloaking her like a queen's robe. Even the tilt of her head and the way she walks speaks of her confidence, the internal knowledge that her makeup is just right.

Within your claws you clutch her flight tendons, slender pistons from inside her body that help the wings take the force of air and weight without collapsing. They remind you that she is, in fact, missing a part of her design.

There's a rustling from above and a moment later Marcus glides down to stand before the slender Siren. He dwarfs her small frame, but she shows no fear as his jasper eyes take her in.

"I believe the last time I saw you, you were broken," he rumbles.

"True." The Siren flares her wings, displaying them with a proud arch of her neck before carefully folding them back around her sides. "Which serves as a telling warning for all of us."

The male sits back on his haunches, a frown lowering his brows. "How so?"

"With the current state of things, if we keep fighting, we'll all end up in the discard heap."

He snorts. "Not if we cow the Discards to stay where they belong."

This time the Siren snorts; it's delicate and full of disdain. "We have far more to lose than they do. I can assure you, they won't be cowed before we pay dearly."

Marcus just stares at her, like this is the first time it's occurred to him how much he has to lose. On the surrounding shelves, there's a nervous rustling of wings and whirring of cogs as dozens of jewel eyes watch the exchange.

Finally, he asks, "What do you propose?"

"I can't believe they agreed!" Eddy whispers against your ear.

You nudge him to give yourself more space while you work on his leg. You're both on top of the workbench. Blain stands guard behind you, but for now you're not too worried. Marcus guaranteed two nights a week for the Discards to emerge from the heap unchallenged.

He refused more because he doesn't want the Maker to notice so many parts missing. It's a fair concern, so you didn't argue when the Siren laid out the terms of the Perfects' agreement. At this rate, you'll have every Discard in functioning condition in about a month.

Like he's reading your mind, Eddy says, "I can't wait." He's gazing up through the skylight where the moon's just starting to disappear from view.

"Soon," you say. The bolt you were

screwing into place snugs into its socket. You return the screwdriver while Eddy tries his leg for the first time. He crows softly in delight.

"Soon," he agrees, "we'll soar the wide world and see what's beyond the shop!"

You share a smile with him and Blain as you all return to the heap. After the negotiations, you brought up with the Discards the question of what happens *after* you all have your parts. None of you believe the Perfects will continue to let the Discards emerge unchallenged indefinitely. So once you have everyone functioning, you'll leave the shop as a group to explore the world.

You gaze up at the skylight as you settle into the heap for the night. Soon. You'll leave soon.

The End

Acknowledgements

This is always one of the best parts for me and also one of the hardest. God has placed so many amazing people in my life and I never feel that a simple thank you in a book is enough to truly express my gratitude.

Thank you first to my beta readers. Mollie, Leslie, Nick, Nate, Mom and Dad, and Myles. Most of you are family and those who aren't may as well be. Which brings up the fact that "they" say not to have family be beta readers. I've never quite followed what "they" say and each one of you brings something to the table, whether that's grammar help, character development, story arc, spotting disappearing torches, or something else. I couldn't do this without amazing people like you.

That brings me to Esther Rohman. I may be gifted in writing, but Esther is gifted with art. She sees the world in a beautiful way and somehow that ends up on paper. Thank you for sharing that gift, Esther.

Alongside Esther is Justin Allen. Justin's work on *Quaking Soul* about made me cry. I couldn't not work with him again on *Discarded Dragons* and he didn't disappoint. He worked to compliment Esther's illustrations and produced a cover I absolutely love. Thank you, thank you, thank you!

Next comes Darren Thornberry. Every time I work with an editor, I'm amazed at the difference it makes for a story. There's just something about that fine tuning that sharpens the writing. Thank you, Darren, for your hard work on *Discarded Dragons*. It's not every day you find an editor excited about your writing.

And last but dearest to my heart is my husband, Nate. You are the best life partner God could have given me. I love you beyond words.

Okay, maybe that wasn't the last one. Thank you as well to my readers. There's a fierce passion among multi-ending Adventure readers and that passion drives me to be better every time I write. Thank you.

Other Books by Jennifer M Zeiger

The Adventure includes three different multi-ending Adventure stories, giving the reader 26 possible endings to find.

Moonrise Mountain: Legend tells of the wild horses that live atop Moonrise Mountain. Now you're out to discover if legend is true, but first, you have to reach the top of the mountain, and each choice you make will bring unforeseen dangers.

Temple of Night and Wind: Many have entered the Howling Maw in search of its treasures. None have returned. But now your village is starving and the Maw's treasures are your last resort. So down into the Maw you venture…

The Tournament: To free your uncle from life in the King's mines, you enter the Tournament. However, this is no typical contest, and its lack of rules makes success all the more difficult and defeat all the more deadly.

Pick wisely, Dear Reader, for success or failure depends on your choices.

This is it. This is Na'rina's chance to prove to her mother and the Dryad Council she can navigate the mythic and human worlds. With night hanging over the city, all she needs to do is sneak in unseen, attend a mythic meeting, and report back. If only she knew who had called the meeting in the first place.

Na'rina is a young Drydanda, destined to be Queen of the Dryads, or tree nymphs. Her world—fauns, nymphs, dwarves—hides in plain sight from the more populated human world. As long as they remain myth, they remain safe.

He's come to warn them but he's a wer-im, a werecat, who was banished centuries ago with the rest of his species for burning the dryad's trees. But humans captured his leader and dozens of other mythical creatures as well. If the mythic world is to survive, he must forge alliances.

When Na'rina's mother goes missing, she finds the violent, banished wer-im her only allies. She soon realizes that everything she's been taught in preparation for leadership appears to be wrong. Who can Na'rina trust while attempting to keep the dryads alive in her mother's absence? As she quickly discovers, the fate of the mythical world rests on her decisions.

Jennifer M Zeiger grew up in the Rocky Mountains of Colorado and now lives in South Carolina with her husband, Nate.

She blogs multi-ending adventure stories and has now turned four of those into books— Three in *The Adventure* and now as a stand-alone, *Discarded Dragons*. She also writes fantasy novels. Check out *Quaking Soul* for the first installment in the Hidden Mythics novels.

jenniferzeiger.com
jennifer.m.zeiger@gmail.com

Note from Jennifer:

Hello Dear Reader. You got to the end of *Discarded Dragons*! I hope you enjoyed it. Whether or not you did, thank you for giving of your valuable time. I am truly blessed to have such a fulfilling job, but I only have that job because of people like you. People kind enough to give my books a chance and spend their hard-earned money buying them. For that I am eternally grateful.

If you enjoyed this book and would like to help, then please consider leaving a review on Amazon, Goodreads, or anywhere else readers visit. The most important part of how well a book sells is how many positive reviews it has, so if you leave one, then you are directly helping me continue on this journey as a full-time writer. Thanks in advance to anyone who does. It means the world to me!

Feel free to contact me. I would love to hear from you.

www.ingramcontent.com/pod-product-compliance
Lightning Source LLC
Chambersburg PA
CBHW021336190726
48288CB00003B/1133